RETRIBUTION

MICHAEL FIORE

Outskirts Press, Inc.
Denver, Colorado

Retribution
All Rights Reserved.
Copyright © 2009 Michael Fiore
v3.0

Cover Photo by Michael Fiore.

Outskirts Press, Inc.
http://www.outskirtspress.com

ISBN: 978-1-4327-3448-0

Outskirts Press and the "OP" logo are trademarks belonging to Outskirts Press, Inc.

PRINTED IN THE UNITED STATES OF AMERICA

Prologue

Beneath a hauntingly luminous moon, Miguel Escobar collapsed on the beach as his only brother, Diego, bleeding unmercifully from a single gunshot wound to his chest , was clinging to life by a single thread. His torso violently heaving. His lungs burning as the last bit of his breath was seeping into the balmy Florida air. A wave of crimson broke out from beneath his once powerful body, turning the white sand beach into a hellish vision that would haunt Miguel for the rest of his days.

With tears streaming down his face and rage building in his heart, Miguel held his brother with all his might. "Everything will be alright. I'm here to take care of you."

Diego stared up at Miguel, his eyes glazing over, unable to say a word. The two brothers pledging devotion to one another in absolute silence.

As the sound of a police siren corrupted the serenity of the waves rolling onto the shore, Diego's body had one last violent tremor before becoming totally still. Miguel screamed at the top of his lungs, vowing to avenge his brother's death.

A Pompano Beach police officer arrived on the scene to find one man shot down in cold blood and another, similar looking man, staring straight into space as he cradled the victim in his arms. His body rocking back and forth at a feverish pace.

Detective Cerniglia was the first to arrive on the scene. He approached the two men with his 9mm drawn, announcing himself as

Pompano Beach Police, cautiously closing the gap between the two men and himself.

"Put your hands on top of your head and slowly get up out of the sand," Cerniglia shouted. There was no response. There was no doubt the man holding the victim was in shock. Cerniglia maintained a safe distance as he waited for backup from both the Pompano Beach Police, as well as the Broward County Sheriff's Department.

He scanned the perimeter of the beach looking for prospective witnesses, weapons and possible perpetrators. The beach seemed deserted. Unusual for this area. The pier at Pompano Beach was normally thriving with groupies following their favorite local bands blasting out guitar rifts and drum solos well into the early morning hours. Not to mention the tourists looking for that romantic moonlight stroll with their loved one. Perhaps just a loved one for that night.

Locals seemed to thrive on young college girls looking for that harmless summer fling. Cerniglia laughed at that thought. Those poor girls usually only found an empty bed in the morning. Maybe a missing wallet. They were the lucky ones. Some ended up with the clap or the nine month blues.

Detective Cerniglia froze. *Was that movement under the pier?* He wanted to check it out, but he could not leave these two here on the beach unattended. Frustrated, he stayed put waiting for backup.

Finally, the quiet was broken by what must have been dozens of sirens, as the reinforcements stormed the beach. The once beautiful moonlit beach now resembled the latest nightclub on the Lauderdale Strip. The strobes of blue lights from the police cruisers, mixing with the spotlights used by the patrolmen to search the area, rivaled the hottest dance floors out there.

After a bit of a struggle, officers finally were able to separate the two men on the beach. Cerniglia put his fingers to the neck of the wounded man feeling for a pulse. Nothing. He wouldn't be able to shed any light on the scene.

The detective approached the other man. He could see the similarity in their faces. He took the wallet from the man's shorts and found out his name was Miguel Escobar. Upon retrieving the stiff's wallet, his hunch was validated. The dead man's name was Diego Escobar. Immediately Cerniglia wondered if these two were the sons of Hector Escobar, leader of the main drug cartel in Miami.

Cerniglia approached the still living Escobar. "What happened here?"

No answer.

"We're gonna have to assume that you killed your brother unless you can tell us otherwise."

Still no response. This guy had lost it. Cerniglia's gut told him that someone else was involved. With no weapon, no clues and a zombie as the only witness, he could see this investigation was pretty much dead in the water.

The County Coroner loaded up Diego's body and headed off for the morgue. Two patrolmen placed Miguel Escobar into the back seat of a Broward County cruiser. He had not uttered a single word since Cerniglia arrived at the scene. No doubt he would end up at the Broward County Psych Center after a trip to the station.

The night returned full circle for Cerniglia as he was alone on the beach once again. He surveyed the beach one last time. There were many questions left unanswered this night. There was, however, one indisputable fact... Miguel Escobar would never be the same.

Chapter 1

May 24, 2006

Frank James found himself trapped once again. His head soaking wet with sweat. He could feel the pools of perspiration collecting under his armpits, leaving huge stains on his favorite Tennessee Vols t-shirt. It had to be his favorite, he'd been wearing it for three days. It was beginning to feel like a second skin.

All of the blinds were closed tightly throughout the house. That didn't seem to matter though. Frank would check them continuously over the next thirty minutes. He had already resorted to tacking up blankets over the sliding glass doors that led to a slab of concrete he called a patio. Paranoia had set in. It always did when he was high. He had an uncanny knack of being able to hear things that weren't there. Peeping through the peep-hole in the front door, he quickly turned an empty coke can on the front lawn into a swat vehicle packed full of snipers just waiting for the Captain's orders to storm this little one bedroom shit-hole he called home.

Frank glanced over at the coffee table in the middle of the living room. Chunks of broken glass, burnt up copper chore, half a dozen lighters, most of which were empty, were scattered all over the table. Everything a mess. Then he saw his prize. He still had three large rocks left. There were ten when he started on this tangent. He'd been at it for three days now.

Fucking crack, he thought. Maybe this would be the day his heart gave out. Although, after years of smoking this evil drug, he seemed to be unable to die. Oh, but how he wished he would have so many times before.

After peeping out the front blinds one last time, Frank hurried over to his futon. He sat down, grabbed his stem and placed a huge boulder on top of the copper. He leaned back, exhaled deeply, sparked up his trusty Bic lighter and brought it to the end of his pipe. The instant popping sound the flame made when it came in contact with the crack sent waves of anticipation through Frank's body. In just a few seconds he would be hearing bells ringing. He inhaled. Slowly at first. Continuing until he was sucking so hard you'd think he was trying to siphon a cantaloupe through a garden hose. The vile smoke filled the chamber of his pipe. He could feel the smoke invading his mouth. His throat. Deep into his lungs. He closed his eyes, preparing for blast off. Just as the rush of his high was coming on full force, the room erupted with an amazingly loud buzzing sound. Was this the end? Was the Blount County Sheriff's Department going to break down the door and put Frank James away for years to come?

The buzzing continued…Frank was stuck. He couldn't run. He couldn't hide. He just sat there until…wham…Frank jumped up off his pillow in a cold sweat. Disoriented. Holding his breath. Finally reaching over and shutting off his alarm clock. He had been dreaming.

Exhaling and wiping the sweat from his brow, James sat in amazement. Next month would be three years that he was clean and sober. Yet, he was still haunted by these nightmares. Drug dreams. That's what they called them at the rehab in Buffalo Valley. He wondered if they would ever stop.

Chapter 2

Frank James rinsed the toothpaste out of his mouth. Splashing water over his face, he caught himself staring in the mirror. He could see his youth starting to fade. His once jet black hair began to be invaded by strands of gray. He began shaving his upper body because it looked as though someone dumped ashes on his chest. He had, however, retained most of the muscle tone from his younger days. One of Frank's goals was to not have the infamous James 'pot belly' become part of his physique.

As he ran his fingers over his freshly shaven face, he stopped and focused on the cleft in his chin. His 'chin-ple'. A combination of chin and dimple. That's what he and Tina used to call it. It was then he realized the importance of today's date. It was May 24th. Tina's birthday. It was also the birthday of his late brother Anthony. Two of the most important people in his life and he had lost them both. Anthony to cancer when he was merely twenty-six years old. Nothing Frank could do about that one. Tina was a different story. It was his own asinine behavior that sent her packing.

Tina Gardner. The one. Never had anyone loved James so much. So unconditionally. That love was returned in equal proportions. For the most part, anyway. When James was clean, he was one of the nicest, most sincere people you would ever want to meet. Dr. Jekyll, so to speak. The minute cocaine entered his system, he became transformed into the evil and hateful Mr. Hyde. He couldn't care about anyone or anything around him.

James had been through several rehabs trying to kick his habit, but they never seemed to stick. Mainly because he took his will back the minute he got home. He would stop going to NA and AA meetings, stop asking for help and he would continue to associate with the same people, places and things that got him into trouble in the first place.

That's what broke Tina's heart. She waited patiently for him to change. And he would. For about three to four weeks at a clip. Then, like clockwork, he would find some feeble excuse to cause him to relapse. It was either 'Tina's too hard on me', or 'work sucks', or 'I was bored'. Some pathetic reason to use drugs.

Well, Tina finally had enough. The day she left sent Frank reeling. He made himself believe it would never come to this. *What a freakin' dreamer!* He went on a two month binge, spending all of his savings, as well as every penny he earned waiting tables at Calhoun's, one of Knoxville's favorite eateries. Then he stopped showing up for work, which finally cost him his job.

He started transporting his dealers around town, sometimes carrying ounces of raw cocaine in his vehicle. He did this to get paid off in crack. James was down to 150 pounds. The man who once prided himself on his appearance was now filthy and unkempt the majority of the time. After several near misses with the law and a drug deal gone bad in South Florida, Frank finally ended up at Blount Memorial Hospital in Maryville, Tennessee because he had no where else to go. He was knocking at death's door. He could barely breathe. That was due to the combination of his chronic asthma and years of smoking crack cocaine. A nearly lethal combination.

From Blount Memorial, he was shipped to Buffalo Valley Addiction Treatment Center in the middle of nowhere in South-Central Tennessee. He spent four weeks there in the intensive inpatient program. After leaving Buffalo Valley, he entered a Half-way House in Nashville, Tennessee. He toughed it out for six months, doing nothing but working on his recovery. What he thought was punishment actually ended up saving his life.

That was two years and eleven months ago. The last time he had touched a drink or a drug. It was also the last time he had seen Tina. Even so, James could still envision her like it was yesterday. Her beautiful blue eyes. That dazzling smile which was usually preceded by the right side of her mouth curling up like Elvis Presley. God she was gorgeous. Her slender frame. Those perfect, perky breasts. And that ass! James used to kid her that there must be a tribe of women somewhere in the world with no asses whatsoever. He was sure that she'd taken their share. Frank could feel the way she melted into him as they lie in bed together. James had not been with a woman since she left. Nobody could compare.

He had stayed in touch with her via letters. Her responses were cordial, but somewhat chilly. She wouldn't allow herself to become vulnerable. It was Frank's goal to win her back. To show her he had changed. He had a future. He wanted to show her that he could support her financially, as well as emotionally. He had spent the last three years doing just that. Today would be the last bit of proof he needed to substantiate his case. He would close the deal he'd been working on for the last eight months. He would finally have his own deli. A life long dream come true.

Chapter 3

Pimento cheese sandwich and tomato soup. Man this food is shit! Miguel Escobar vowed to never eat a sandwich or tomato soup ever again. No grilled cheese, hot dogs or tuna casserole either, for that matter. Anything that would remind him of this hell-hole would be off limits to him.

Three years. Three excruciatingly long years he had been trapped in the maximum security ward of the Broward County Psych Center. Three years of ping pong, 'B' movies and chaperoned visits. Three years away from his family. No doubt the worst of it all was the fact that the man who killed his brother had a three year head start to disappear and never be brought to justice.

Brought to justice. Miguel laughed even though the situation was not the least bit humorous. He laughed because Webster's definition of justice would not even remotely match his. His justice was actually revenge. Death. That is the only way Miguel could get past what happened on the beach three years ago. The only thing that could give him a ghost of a chance to have what most would call a normal life.

No time for feeling sorry for himself. He had three years to do that if he so chose. That would have been unproductive. Miguel had more important things to do. He had to learn how to act. He was under close scrutiny by the staff of the ward. The Judge had made it clear that he was not to be released until the anger and thoughts of revenge had absolutely disappeared. Since that wasn't likely to happen, Miguel had to be extremely convincing playing the part of a reformed, forgiving man.

Apparently he had done well thus far, because today was his hearing in front of the Board of Appeals. Oh, how he had waited for this moment. After his pathetic excuse for a lunch, Escobar would head back to his room to put on the finishing touches. Miguel's family had brought him all of the articles of clothing he had asked for, complete with accessories. If he was going to play the part, he needed to look the part.

After shaving, Miguel put on the khaki Dockers he had chosen. He matched those with a conservative white, cotton button-down Oxford. Dark brown, wing-tipped Mephisto shoes, a plain brown belt and a yellow power tie brought together the entire college boy image he was going for. A pair of wire-framed, John Lennon style glasses completed the ensemble.

Miguel checked himself out in front of the full-length mirror on the back of his door for what seemed like an eternity. The corners of his mouth began to curl upwards. He was truly pleased. Lights! Cameras! Action!

Chapter 4

There was a light tapping on his door. "Come in," he responded.

The door opened slowly. In walked Dr. Vernon. Miguel could feel his pulse quicken. Here was the woman with which he had spent the majority of his time during his three year tenure here at Shangri-La. He shared with her intimate details of his life that no one else in the world was privy to. That alone was enough to excite him, but there was more. Long, shapely legs. Auburn hair that swept across her face with each graceful turn of her head. Sparkling green eyes that reminded him of the sea that pounded the rocks at his favorite fishing spot back home in Puerto Rico.

"Are you ready Miguel?" she asked.

"I think so, but I'm a little scared. I'm sure that I couldn't get through this without your guidance and support."

"I'm sure you'll do just fine. Be yourself. Tell them the truth and this will all be over quickly. You've come a long way, Miguel. You should be proud of yourself. I am. You've dealt with some very deep issues while you were here. We'll continue to see each other weekly as planned, so it's not like you're going to be all by yourself when you get out. I'll be here for you whenever you need me."

For a doctor, she's awfully gullible. Miguel couldn't believe how easy this was going to be. "Okay, let's get this over with."

Miguel drank up one more lustful look at those incredible legs, got off his bed and stepped out into the hallway. Showtime! He would have to remember to do something nice for Dr. Vernon. After all, she was his passport to freedom.

Chapter 5

As James drove down Alcoa Highway on his way to Knoxville, he was finally able to get a grip on his nervousness about closing the deal. He knew he put together a very strong plan. This was no spontaneous pipe dream that was the norm back in his using days. How many crazy schemes did he come up with back then? Thousands. He even came up with some legitimate ideas. Some pretty sure fire money making ideas. But… he was using. As long as he used, he would never act on any of these ideas. Wasted opportunities.

He played the deal over and over in his head. James realized he wasn't really nervous about the plan. The plan was solid. It went much deeper than that. He was unsure of himself. Well, he was going to see the one person that could get him back on track.

Mark Length was an unforgettable character. He and James had been through many an adventure together. His oldest and dearest friend. He was Frank's general manager at the first restaurant that gave him a management opportunity. Uncle Bud's Catfish in Knoxville, back in 1992. Mark took him under his wing and the two of them had been inseparable since.

Mark was a thinker. A planner. The only difference between Mark and James was that Mark took action to make his plans come to life. He was a drinker, but never let it control him. He could never figure out how James could let drugs take over his whole life. While he didn't agree with the way James chose to live his life at times, he never turned his back on his troubled friend. Every time they were reunited, it was as if they were never apart.

James passed by Hoo-Ray's and Manhattan's and finally pulled into the parking lot behind Spicy's. Spicy's was Mark Length's restaurant. James had been the general manager until a week ago. He left because he needed to devote himself totally to his own project. Length supported him one hundred percent. James was his protégé. A work in progress. He could keep an eye on James to make sure he crossed all the T's and dotted all the I's.

James walked up the ramp and used his own key to enter the building. The familiar smell of the place overwhelmed him, bringing back all kinds of memories. The smell of stale beer and chicken wings. God, how he loved that smell. Spicy's was like no other place he'd been involved with before. To say it was eclectic wouldn't amount to the tip of the iceberg. The walls were splattered with ceramic versions of real life tattoos. Mark's idea. He loved tattoos. He had hundreds of pictures of them on his computer. It had to be pretty original or meaningful in some cosmic way to make the 'Wall of Fame.'

The bar was mahogany and shaped like a boomerang. The significance of the boomerang was that Mark thought people, like boomerangs, would keep coming back. The walls behind the bar were red, with one black door leading to the CO_2 tanks that powered the kegs. When Mark took over the building, that door was red as well. Mark, however, was compelled to paint it black because of a segment of the popular Door's tune, 'I see a red door and I want to paint it black.' Mark certainly danced to the beat of a different drummer. James loved him for it.

Spicy's was a hot spot for late night activity in the Old City, Knoxville's trendy neighborhood that was home to several clubs and restaurants. Frank smiled as he reflected back on how many times he had to kick out thirty or more people, on any given night, at three in the morning. He became an Old City icon because of his usual closing statement, "If you ain't working here or banging me…you gotta get the hell outta here!"

As Frank stood at the bar waiting for Mark to realize that he was there, he wondered to himself if his place would have the same type of charisma and unforgettable characters that were inherent to Spicy's.

Chapter 6

"What up Dick?" That had been Mark's greeting ever since he and Frank became friends.

"Nuttin' Dick. What up with you?" Frank's standard reply.

"Shouldn't you be practicing your spiel for the investors?"

"Shit…if I don't know it by now I'm in trouble. I do know it…right?"

Mark laughed. "Is that what this is all about? You want ol' Mark to comfort you in your time of need?"

"Not if you mean comfort me like you did in Chattanooga. By sitting on my chest and making me smoke pot until I was a freakin' vegetable."

"Desperate times call for desperate measures, Dick!"

"Well, I'm not that desperate." James inhaled deeply and let it out slowly. "I just keep wondering if I'm ready. Ya know? This is the major leagues. I mean… I'm a freakin' drug addict for crying out loud."

Mark jumped off his stool and got right in Frank's face. "That's not what you are. It's just something you did. You've got to move on. Stop with all that self-pity bullshit." Length wasn't one to candy coat things. That's probably the reason James went to see him in the first place. "It's almost been what, three years?"

James looked at Length as if he had three heads. *He remembered.*

"What? You don't think I keep track of that shit? What am I? You must think I'm just some freak that cares solely about money and strippers."

"Aren't you?"

"Well, yeah. But that's just a part of me. After all we've been through? I keep track of you. I care. I know damn well that next month is three years clean for you."

"I know you care. You don't have to tell me. I guess I'm just used to people giving up on me."

"Not me. Never happen." Mark went around the bar and poured a couple of cokes. "Frank, you're ready. You don't even realize just how ready you are. For the last two years you have been a business owner. You took ownership of my business. I didn't have to worry about anything at all."

"Yeah, but I could always call you when I didn't know something."

"So! What makes you think that has to change? I'll always be there for you."

Mark gave Frank a hug. A short one because Mark prided himself on not being sensitive. He said he was a natural man. He despised all those tree-hugging, poetry-reading, artsy types that believe it is perfectly natural for men to show their feminine sides whenever they felt the urge. "Just be yourself. Trust in yourself. You can definitely do this."

Chapter 7

The tension that had once been unbearable now seemed like something from the distant past. However, James wasn't about to show his elation. Not here. He was determined to show the board there was never any question that this deal would go through. Inside, however, he felt fireworks comparable to the Fourth of July finale exploding throughout his body.

His dream was coming true. Just like his fellowship had promised. He was proud of all he had accomplished in the last three years. There were a lot of doubters. Most of whom were the people closest to him. His father, step father and sister leading the pack.

Would this finally make me believable in their eyes?, James wondered. It really didn't matter either way. Frank had conditioned himself to not be bothered by other people's negativity. Buying in on that garbage was one of the main things that kept him using drugs in the old days. Through the fellowship of Alcoholics Anonymous, James had learned that he had to live to make himself happy. He realized now that he had no control over others opinions and that, in their eyes, he would always come up short in regards to their expectations. That failure and lack of acceptance would keep him in a constant state of impending doom. Today, he tried to live up to his goals and expectations. The result of which had become a life dominated by serenity and self-confidence as opposed to being restless, irritable and full of discontent.

Finally, with all the handshakes and slapping of backs

completed, Frank headed out to his car. His old car. That was one of the things he planned to change first. He needed a new ride. Something that would allow him to lug around everything from restaurant equipment to hamburger meat to dining room tables and chairs. James had seen a black, metallic Ford F150 the other day that would perfectly suit his needs. His Chrysler Concorde simply would not do.

Frank smiled at the thought of his Concorde, knowing full well that he would never part with it. Too much sentimental value. He had bought that car from his old college roommate, Hadley. This was back a few years when he was working in Lake George, New York. He moved to upstate New York to try a geographical cure for his drug addiction. Hadley sold him the car for fifteen hundred dollars. It was worth twice that. Hadley was a true friend. Always in Frank's corner. Come to think of it…James had never finished paying that car off. He would definitely have to rectify that.

James got in the car and took off down Kingston Pike toward Spicy's. Mark had to be the first to know the good news. As James got closer to the University of Tennessee campus, he was overcome with the feeling that he was being followed. He quickly changed lanes, just as Kingston Pike turned into Cumberland Avenue. 'The Strip' as it was known to the thousands of orange-clad soldiers that packed Cumberland Avenue for every Vol's home football game.

Frank began to zigzag through the traffic while keeping his eyes in the rearview mirror. He couldn't be certain, but it appeared as though a large, black sports utility vehicle was mimicking his every move. With the Strip being a high volume traffic area, he decided to give the SUV a test. He slowed down as he approached Seventeenth Street, waited for the light to turn red and immediately took a hard left on Seventeenth, barely missing the oncoming traffic.

Amidst the sounds of protesting car horns, Frank pulled to the side of the road to see the reaction, if any, of the man driving the SUV. The driver of what turned out to be a Cadillac Escalade with Florida plates had his eyes glued on James as he beat the steering wheel with frustration.

Suspicion confirmed. *Who the hell could that be?,* Frank

curiously wondered. He had worked hard over the last three years to not make any enemies. That didn't necessarily mean he hadn't. Then again, there was always the possibility of his sordid past catching up with him. James shook his head. He would have to worry about all this later. Right now he had some fantastic news that could not wait to be shared.

Chapter 8

Miguel Escobar squinted into the bright Florida sunshine. It had been almost three years since he stood outside the gates of the Broward County Psych Center. His performance in front of the Board of Appeals rivaled any number of Oscar-caliber performances of the past. Freedom at last.

Somehow the air felt fresher, smelled sweeter and the sun was warmer and more comforting than he'd ever remembered. It warmed him to the bone, something it had been unable to do in the three years he spent inside. He was sure it was due to his new found freedom. As Miguel became acclimated to the sun, he started scanning the parking lot for familiar faces. He was hoping to see his family. Everything inside him, however, told him it would not happen. They would surely send some flunkies to pick him up. Hector Escobar, head of the largest and most powerful drug cartel in South Florida, was much too busy to perform such menial tasks. Regardless of the fact that Miguel was his only remaining son.

Out of the corner of his eye, Miguel noticed a brand new Lincoln Towncar pulling off of Sample Road. It turned into the parking lot and headed straight for Miguel. As the Lincoln came to a halt right in front of Miguel, a smile broke out across his face as he recognized his good friend Sandoval. Sandoval and Miguel had been running together since they were in diapers. With Diego gone, Sandoval was the closest thing Miguel had to a brother.

Sandoval was taken in by Hector Escobar when his mother and father were killed by some Haitians trying to move in on Hector's turf. Hector vowed to avenge the grisly murders. He also vowed to take care of his good friend's son. A few weeks later, the Miami Police began finding pieces of human remains throughout Little Haites, a *barrio* in Miami predominately made up of Haitian refugees. After a prolonged investigation, the police pieced together the puzzle. The sum of the body parts added up to be the two Haitian militants suspected in the murders of Antonio and Carmen Melendez. Sandoval's parents.

Sandoval hugged Miguel with all his might. It was truly a blessing to have his *hermano*, his brother, back with him at last. "I have some news for you," Sandoval smiled.

"I knew I could count on you my old friend."

"I have sent Javier and Troncillo to keep tabs on your old friend Frank James."

"Where is he exactly?"

"Knoxville, Tennessee. Well, he lives in a small town called Maryville, but spends the majority of his time in Knoxville."

"What else?"

Sandoval grinned. "I believe we've discovered that he's got family living in Maryville as well."

Miguel's brain was reeling. He felt electricity pumping throughout his entire body. *Revenge,* he thought. He began to fantasize about spilling the blood of that bastard's entire family. He would kill ten people to make up for the death of his brother. "You have done well Sandoval. You will be rewarded greatly for this."

"My reward will be seeing this James character hung up by his *cajones*." Sandoval grabbed his crotch as he said this, sharing a hearty laugh with Miguel.

Sandoval's cell phone rang. "*Hola.* I don't want to hear you lost him. I want to know his every move. Everyone he's come in contact with. Do not disappoint me on this. *Adios.*"

Miguel's face began to go flush. "Is there a problem?"

"No. No problem. They had been following him this morning. Apparently he had a meeting with some investors. Javier said everyone seemed to be happy. He thinks James got the backing he needed for some sort of restaurant or deli that he's been trying to open. They lost him around the University of Tennessee campus. Not to worry, though. We know where he lives."

"A restaurant. This is good news. It gives me an idea." Miguel ran his bony fingers across his chin. "Did Javier say if they had been spotted by James?"

"*Si*. He said James pulled over and stared straight at him."

"Tell them to back off. We don't want our pigeon to fly the coop. Have them sit tight at the hotel and wait for further instructons."

Sandoval dialed the phone and barked out his orders. After snapping his cell phone together, he turned to Miguel and said, "Done. What now, *Jefe*?"

"Now? We go home and pack. What's the weather like in Tennessee anyway?" Miguel smiled. Yes... he had a good plan. No time to waste. "We leave in the morning."

Chapter 9

James pulled his car into Spicy's parking lot once again. *Déjà vu,* he thought. Once again he climbed the ramp to the back door. As he entered through the back, he heard familiar voices. Normally he would not have thought twice. These voices, however, should not have been at Spicy's at this particular time of day.

He turned the corner by the dart machines and stopped dead in his tracks. *Fuckin' Mark,* he said to himself as he stood with his hands on his hips, shaking his head. As he looked out toward the dining room, a crowd of people were staring at him with shit-eating grins. Above the bar was a large banner that said 'OPENING SOON…THE KNUCKLE SANDWICH DELI.' Mark truly had faith in James. He had organized a little congratulations party. As Frank looked around the room, he saw all of the faces that were important and influential in his life.

Sitting at the bar were the boys from the tattoo parlor. *Some things never change.* Frank always wondered how that business stayed open. Who the hell were doing the tattoo's? These guys were always here. Johnny Tattoo was drinking his usual triple screwdriver. He was probably Frank's favorite. When he got drunk he did an awesome Robert DeNiro impression. Next to him were Marcus and Daniel. Frank thought that they must had been Siamese twins in another life. You would never see one without the other. Trailing the pack, as usual, was Melanie. She was Marcus' girl. Well, she was every other day after they made up. They were constantly brawling. Marcus usually got so mad that he would wait for her to pass out so he could tattoo her somewhere she would not have agreed to if she were coherent in the least. That was his motus operandi.

One day in particular stood out in his mind. This time he took his spitefullness to a whole other level. Melanie stormed into Spicy's looking for Marcus with murder in her eyes, cursing and slamming things around. Frank heard the commotion all the way from the kitchen. When he got in the dining room, he could see that she was making a spectacle of herself. Frank grabbed her. He took her into the office and proceeded to find out what was wrong. It turned out that while she was unconscious, Marcus tattooed *'cockpit'* inside her bottom lip. Fearing a beating and trying to be sensitive to Melanie's situation, Frank had to control the hysteria dying to part from his lips. Frank stood in amazement. You truly see something new everyday in this damn business.

Frank looked at the table closest to the bar. It was crowded with pitchers of soda, cups, napkins, chicken wings and a cake in the shape of a boxing glove. Scribbled across the cake in red lettered frosting were the words 'Knuckle Sandwich'.

Gathered around the table were several of Frank's pals from Alcoholics Anonymous. Bret, Jimmy Joe, Megan and his sponsor, Carl Metcalf. Each of their faces beaming with pride over the success of another recovering addict. Another miracle.

"Uncle Frankie! Uncle Frankie!"

Frank knew that voice. His little sweetheart. The girl that melted his heart with just one glance. His niece Rachel. She took off in a full sprint, leaping into Frank's arms. With her arms and legs wrapped around his waist, she began showering him with sweet kisses.

James felt two hands cover his eyes from behind. He had a pretty good idea who that was too. "Tyler, is that you?"

"Hey Frankie". He was a big boy now, so he dropped 'Uncle'. Frank didn't mind. "Can I have a job?"

"How about manager?"

"Yeah! Hey Mom...Frankie said I get to boss you around."

Tyler took off like a shot. He headed back over to the Indy Car racing game. Frank laughed at the fact that Tyler had been like that as long as he could remember. Any shiny object and he immediately forgot what he was doing.

Frank turned back to the group just in time to see his sister making her way over to him. Rose James was five years older than Frank. She was in the midst of battling Multiple Sclerosis. She was a single mom. Even though the kid's father was still in the picture, Rose was left with a majority of their upbringing. Frank had helped look after the three of them on and off for several years now. Frank and Rose had been pretty tight over the years, despite a subtle ongoing competition for their mother's affection that had seen the two do ruthless things to one another. Frank used to harbor severe resentments toward his sister that allowed him to wallow in self pity and continue his drug use. He worked hard on those resentments over the past three years. Today he realized that she couldn't be held responsible for the things she had said and done. She was in the throws of addiction herself. Her addiction was brought on by the mass quantities of prescription drugs given to her by the many physicians trying to keep her Multiple Sclerosis under control.

"I'm proud of you, baby brother," Rose said as she gave him a bear hug.

"Yeah, I'm kinda proud of myself. I can't believe it's finally happening."

"You've worked hard for it. Nobody gave any of this to you."

"I can't wait to call Mom. Dad too, for that matter. I'll bet he'll be shocked. I wasn't supposed to amount to anything."

After getting a chance to mix and mingle with all the party guests, Mark turned the music down and stood on the bar. "I've known this son-of-a-bitch for some time now. I've seen him at the top. I've seen him in the pits of hell. I've loved him. I've hated him. I've even wanted to beat his ass. But today, justice was served. Frank, our hats are off to you. You've been given a gift. I personally have no doubt that you will knock 'em dead." Mark raised his glass. "To Frank James...my very best friend."

The crowd roared. The music came back on. The rest of the afternoon was spent dancing, playing pool and shootin' the shit.

Chapter 10

"Hello."

There was a moment of silence.

"Hello? Anyone there?"

"Hey Tina. It's me…Frank."

"I know who it is. What do you want?"

Ouch! Not a good start, Frank thought to himself. He continued on. No pain, no gain. "I wanted to share some good news with you. I got the financing yesterday. The Knuckle Sandwich Deli is going from dream to reality."

"That's great Frank. Really great."

"I thought maybe you'd like to see the spot I've got picked out. I can't imagine anyone else being the first to see it."

Another stretch of silence. "I don't know if that's such a good idea."

"Why not? What have you got to lose?"

"What do I have to lose? Are you serious? Have you forgotten how much you hurt me? You made me cry so fuckin' much I ran out of tears! The lies. The drugs. It's not something I can just forget."

"I'm not asking you to forget. I just thought…"

"I know what you thought. That getting your own place was gonna make me jump right back into your arms."

"No! That's not it."

"Then what, Frank? What were you thinking?"

"I don't know. I guess maybe that you could atleast forgive me. I've been working really hard to change. I just don't see why you can't give me a chance."

"I am giving you a chance. I didn't hang up on your ass…did I?"

"No, but…"

"No fucking buts! Listen. I'm real proud of you for getting this deal. I'm even more proud of you for staying clean. I know you've been working hard. Maybe I will forgive you. But that's on my time, not yours. Just because you've changed doesn't mean that everyone you hurt is going to jump up and down and act like nothing ever happened. Your life has changed. But I would hope you changed for you. Not for me or anyone else. So just do what you have to do for yourself. Stop trying to control everything and relax. Let things work themselves out. That's God's job. Let Him do it."

"I know how much I've hurt people, Tina. You in particular. I know that sometimes I try to rush things. It's just the whole time I've been working on this thing, I imagined sharing it with you. I love you, Tina. Always have. And I did change for myself. But, I never stopped having faith that we would be together again. So, I'm gonna keep pursuing you. You're just gonna have to keep turning me down. I'll be patient. I see us together again. I believe in it. So take all the time you need to get your feelings straight. I'll wait. I've been waiting. I've not seen anyone since we've been apart. You're my Angel, baby! Nobody else can compare."

Frank choked back the tears. This kind of thing would have thrown him for a loop in the past. There definitely would be an AA meeting in his future tonight.

"Well, I hope I didn't upset you too much T. I guess I'll talk to you another time. I love you, baby. Good-bye."

"Frank? Frank?"

"Yeah?"

"Maybe I could be the first one to get something to eat at your place. Stay in touch."

Hope is a beautiful thing!

Chapter 11

S andoval turned to Miguel as the 747 descended into Maghee-Tyson Airport in Alcoa, Tennessee. "There's no buildings. What in the hell have we gotten ourselves into?"

"Relax, *companiero*, I promise the wild animals will not get you. Besides, it's the rednecks you need to worry about. I hear they tie you up and make you watch NASCAR."

"Fuck that! I'm staying at the hotel."

The two men shared a laugh as they pulled into the gate. They gathered their carry-ons from above and began to be herded out of the plane like cattle. As they cleared the ramp and entered the main terminal, they saw Javier standing by a magazine rack.

The three men shook hands and headed to baggage claim. They would not talk business in the airport. Someone could overhear them. It was not probable, but Miguel would do nothing to risk their mission.

Once the baggage was collected, they strode toward the parking area. There was the Escalade. It would be alright for the ride from the airport, but they would have to make other arrangements for transportation now that the SUV had been made by James near the UT campus.

"Javier. Tomorrow you will rent a car for your stakeouts. Something inconspicuous with Tennessee tags. Then I want you to show me around the area. I need to know where James lives, where his family lives, the bar he used to work at and the location of this new business he's about to open. Tranquillo and Sandoval...your job is to travel up and down this highway to find me a car. Something beat up. High miles. Then we will meet back at the room. I will explain my plan and the parts each of you will play. That is tomorrow. Tonight…a good meal, drinks and I would like to sample some of this southern hospitality I have heard so much about. It's been three years since I've touched a woman's flesh. I am not lying to you my friends…I need some *chocha*!"

Javier looked at Miguel in the back seat. "And plenty of pussy you shall have, *Jefe*. I found a place in Knoxville called the Katch One. Very friendly girls and they like to party. Tranquillo and I have become familiar there, so we get special treatment."

"Very well. Tonight we feast. Tomorrow, however, we get down to business."

Chapter 12

Frank James pulled into the parking lot of UT Hospital. As he drove up to the automatic ticket machine, he realized he wasn't fond of all aspects of modern technology. *What was so bad about having a living and breathing human being give you a ticket and say hello?* Too much technology in areas it wasn't needed was one of the reasons why communication skills among people were going in the toilet. He was a 'people' person since he was a kid. He loved the interaction with different people. The restaurant business had only strengthened his love for people. Their opinions. Their experiences. Their quirks.

Then came cocaine. At first, the drug made him the life of the party. Snorting coke and drinking were done in a casual nature. He could do anything when he used them. There wasn't a woman he couldn't get, a man he couldn't defeat or an adversary he couldn't make a believer. He was 'ten feet tall and bullet proof'.

The drugs accented the good points of his personality and had virtually no negative effects. He ran million dollar corporate restaurants. He was called upon to open several new restaurants and was responsible for the training of both the service and kitchen staffs. The corporate higher-ups would often ask him to go to a location that wasn't performing up to snuff and rectify the situation. James would go in and observe the day to day operations and see if the speed of service was lacking, the quality of food was off or perhaps the staff wasn't as spirited or motivated as it should be. All of this affected sales and had a direct impact on the bottom line.

All was not sunshine and roses for very long. First, he started increasing the amounts and frequency of use. His judgement and overall performance began to suffer. He began putting himself in risky situations. Hangovers became a daily obstacle. Soon, sleep became harder and harder to come by. Then it stopped all together. Three and four day binges became the norm. Sober workdays became a thing of the past. He started staying at work after hours, drinking with his staff. Harmless at first. Soon, the place turned into an after hours joint that featured an open bar. Finally, James compromised his managerial integrity by sleeping with several female members of his staff.

In the final stages of his addiction, James found the morals and beliefs he was raised with had virtually evaporated. Doing things that were inconceivable became common occurrences. He replaced the people in his life that had values with ruthless, self-centered creatures of the night. He let drug dealers use him for crack. His home would be invaded as the dealers needed a place to cook down their raw cocaine. They would leave the place trashed and smelling like shit from the many blounts they rolled and smoked. They smoked like locomotives as they scurried around cooking, cutting and bagging their poison to sell to men, women and children from all walks of life.

Then came the vultures. Men and women that had a sixth sense about cocaine. They knew when someone had it and exactly where they were. Guys would show up at James house with small amounts of crack to get them in the door, expecting to stay until the plate of crack left by the dealers was gone. When Frank told them to leave, they would get pissed and end up trying to steal anything that wasn't bolted down.

Even more pitiful were the women. They had no shame. They would come to the house prepared to have themselves violated in unspeakable ways. James couldn't count the offers of oral sex, threesomes and any other freaky sexual scenarios that one could imagine. That, fortunately, was the one value James held onto. He couldn't bring himself to disrespect these poor souls. He couldn't stand to see those women do degrading things for crumbs of crack. He would usually share with them so they didn't have to defile themselves for a fix. Frank knew it was only a temporary hiatus for these kind of girls. As soon as he was out of drugs, they were sure to move onto the next host.

The final stages of addiction were where hard times came into play. Loneliness, fear, guilt and shame were emotions that ran rampant in James' mind. Jails and institutions became where he took up residence. The courts got tired of seeing his face. The police were instantly on alert when his name was mentioned. His car was known. He frequently had to find other ways to get in and out of the 'Hood' and other high risk areas.

Work became a thing of the past. He could niether hold a job, nor did he have the desire to get a job. Scheming and hustling became his way of life. Dishonesty and selfishness became his creed. People left skid marks when he approached. He wasn't allowed in most people's houses because he became one of the vultures he despised. His family opted not to see him. They could barely stomach his voice when he called because of the heartache and sorrow it would cause them. James' mother, who had always been his best friend and confidant, was hurt so badly that she said some words that he would never be able to forget. She said, "I'll always love you because you're my son. But right now I don't like you one stinkin' bit!"

Frank got out of the Concorde, locked the door and just stood for a moment. He inhaled the warm Tennessee air deeply into his lungs. He slowly exhaled and headed for the hospital. He needed to talk to someone. Someone that would understand. Someone that had been there. Someone in Alcoholics Anonymous. Tears rolled down his cheeks as he scurried toward the auditorium where the meeting was being held.

Chapter 13

Carl Metcalf was a character right out of the movie 'Grumpy Old Men'. Every time Frank looked at him he was reminded of the grandfather, played by Burgess Meredith. He had told Carl that on many occasions. Except for the fact that the grandfather was ninety four, Carl took it as a compliment. Metcalf was a wiry, feisty Irishman. At five years of age, he had seen his share of calamity. He grew up in the streets of Belfast, Ireland. By the age of sixteen, Metcalf was an expert rifleman and was well on his way to becoming one of the most feared demolitions men in Ireland. All of Europe, for that matter. Never really having a shot at being a normal youth, he had lost his childhood when he picked up his first weapon at the age of nine. A Walther PPK that his father kept in the house for protection. Two Protestants invaded his home and attacked his sister. Carl snuck down the stairs and put two bullets in each man's back.

When Carl's father returned home, he beamed with pride over what his fine young son had done. A true Metcalf he was. He grabbed the bottle of Irish Whiskey in the cupboard over the sink and he brought it over to the kitchen table. He called his son to him. Carl, still unaware of what he had done, scurried over to his father's side. Terry Metcalf filled two glasses and looked his son square in the eyes. He praised Carl for the bravery he showed and told him that tonight he became a man. They raised their glasses and toasted their good health. That was the beginning of the worst battle of Carl's life. The bloodshed, chaos and death to follow would keep Carl looking to the bottle to cover up the pain and misery that became what his life was all about.

By the age of thirty, Carl had already seen more atrocities against the human spirit than any one man should be subjected to. His constant drinking made him lose the edge he once had. Alcoholic tremors made him miss as many targets as he hit. He couldn't concentrate. His nerves were continuously frazzled. After several close calls with both his and his family's lives, Carl made a decision to escape the hell he called home. He sold everything they had and came to America.

After settling in Knoxville, Tennessee in 1971, Carl became acquainted with a group of gentlemen that seemed to understand him very well. They had told Carl their own life stories. Wars. Depression. Alcoholic bliss. The similarities were astounding. They explained to him the steps they had taken to overcome their obsession with alcohol. This peaked both Carl's interest and curiosity. He began to attend gatherings where a group of people got together to share common experiences and problems with the goal of finding workable solutions. The gatherings were meetings of Alcoholics Anonymous. Carl was told that if he remained honest with himself and others, he would be able to have a life beyond his wildest dreams. Honesty, along with openmindedness and the ability to take suggestions, could relieve him of the bondage of alcohol. It had been thirty five years since Carl had indulged in any type of mind altering substance. He was living proof that the program of Alcoholics Anonymous worked.

He freely gave away what was given to him by other members of the group. Once the student, he was now the teacher. His biggest challenge was Frank James.

Chapter 14

Frank had the gait of a death row inmate as he approached the crowd out side the auditorium doors. Head down, shoulders slouched and a slow, trepidatious march toward the group. His peers could tell at once that there was something troubling their friend. It had been some time since they had seen James this far down in the dumps.

Carl Metcalf was the first one to reach Frank. Being Frank's sponsor, Carl had seen many occasions where he had looked so down and out. As a matter of fact, there were stretches where James would string together weeks at a time filled with depression and despair. They were long ago, back when Frank first entered the program. He had made major strides in his recovery since then. However, this program doesn't guarantee that there will not be bad days. It simply tells us that we need not drink or use drugs to deal with life today.

"What's on yer mind, Frank?" Carl gave James a bear hug. "You look like shit!"

"I don't know", Frank said sheepishly.

"Who in the hell ya think yer talkin' to? You forgetting I was the one listening to your bitchin' and moanin' the entire first year your sorry ass was here?"

Frank cracked a little grin. He should have known better than to try and pull the wool over his sponsor's eyes. He hadn't been able to do that since the day he met him.

"I called her today."

"By her I'm guessing you mean Tina?"

"Yeah."

Carl smiled. Frank had not been able to give up on the chance of reconciliation with Tina. He still hadn't decided if that was good or bad. But, Carl did know that there was nothing he or anyone else could do to change Frank's mind. "What happened? Did she answer this time?"

"She did answer. I was psyched. Then she hammered me. She said she knew I was trying to change, but that didn't mean she had to forgive me for all the shit I'd done."

"Good for her."

"That's really not what I wanted to hear."

"Too damn bad! I'm not here to tell you what you *want* to hear. I'm here to tell you what you *need* to hear."

"I know that you old bastard. Let me finish." Frank took a deep breath, held it for a few seconds, then exhaled. "I told her I still love her. That she could take all the time she needed."

"And what did she have to say to that?" This was always the part that worried Carl. Would she say something to push Frank over the edge? He put his feelings out there and left himself completely vulnerable in the process.

"She didn't say anything."

"Uh oh," Carl thought to himself.

"At first. Then, when I was about to hang up she called out my name. She told me to keep in touch. Maybe she could be the first one to eat at my place."

Carl waited for the disastrous part of the conversation. It never came. He laughed. *This one should be easy*, he thought. "So…what's the damn problem?

That sounded like a pretty good call. Hell fire, boy! She told you to keep in touch for cryin' out loud."

"That's just it. After all I've done to her. I was horrible. I lied. I stole and couldn't be depended on. Yet she still wants me to stay in touch."

"That's what you want, dumbass! She has to forgive you in order for you two to get back together. Sounds to me like she's startin' to do just that."

"But why?"

"She obviously still has hope for you. She must see something in you that you can't…or won't. You can't stay guilty over the shit you did while you were using. Forgiveness isn't just for others. As a matter of fact, it starts with ourselves."

Frank bowed his head. "Sometimes it's just so hard. Sometimes I'm unsure of how to forgive myself. How to forgive anyone for that matter."

Metcalf crossed his arms and cocked his head. "I guess tonight you start at square one. Get your ass into that meeting, bring up the topic of forgiveness and listen to what people did to forgive. Just listen! When you get home, get out the Big Book and read the story called 'Freedom From Bondage.' Then hit your knees and ask the good Lord for help. If that don't work, call me. 'Cause if that don't work, the only thing left is for me to stick my boot straight up yer ass!"

Frank shook his head and headed into the auditorium. He could feel his self-pity subsiding. Carl had that effect on him. He was always a bull in a china shop when it came to Frank's feelings. Apparently, that's what James needed. Every time.

The rest of the evening went as planned. Frank and Carl took a seat. Frank brought up the topic of forgiveness. He listened. The meeting ended and they said their good-byes. Frank got in his car and headed back down Alcoa Highway. He had a date with the Big Book. He knew damn well that Carl would be calling first thing in the morning to quiz him on his 'homework.'

Frank truly felt blessed with the people in his life today. They cared for him sincerely. Still, he had to believe the best was yet to come.

Chapter 15

Miguel, Sandoval, Javier and Tranquillo slouched in their seats as James passed by them in the UT Hospital parking lot. When they were sure they had gone unnoticed, the Escalade roared to life. They circled slowly through the lot, careful not to be seen by the hard looking old man they were scouting. Miguel watched Metcalf get into his PT Cruiser and quickly wrote down his tag number. Escobar believed he had found one of the casualties he would need to carry out his plan for revenge.

"Let's go." Miguel motioned to Javier to leave. "I'm getting very hungry."

"Where to *Jefe?*"

"I read about this place in the hotel lounge called Calhoun's On The River. I think I would like to start there."

Tranquillo spoke from the back seat. "I have been there, *Jefe*. It is very nice. Head toward Knoxville. Follow I-40 until you get to the Summit Hill Drive exit. Take a left at the light and we will run right into it."

Calhoun's On The River was a mammoth structure on the banks of the Tennessee River. Constantly bustling with patrons from open to close, Calhoun's was a favorite of locals, businessmen and tourists alike. It was also home to the Vol Navy. Throughout the Tennessee Vol's football season, the entire river would be jammed up with boatfuls of maniacal Volunteer fans. They began docking at Calhoun's at dawn on football Saturdays. After a half dozen hours of tailgating, the throngs of alcohol-riddled fans would make the pilgramage to

Neyland Stadium. A sea of orange unlike anything you have ever seen.

Miguel immediately took a liking to the place. Decorated with dark paneled walls, bronze fixtures and soft lighting, it made one immediately feel relaxed and welcome. Sandoval gave the hostess his name and the four men decided to wait at the bar.

The lounge area consisted of a large rectangular mahogany bar surrounded by several tall tables and chairs. Every inch of the bar was packed full of a wide range of characters. Everything from power business meetings to fraternity boys drinking yards of draft beer to thirty-something women on the prowl, looking for Mr. Right...or at least Mr. Right Now.

All eyes focused on the four well-dressed Hispanic men approaching the bar. As advanced as this city was, it didn't take much to bring out the red-neck in people. In their eyes, Hispanics worked on their farms and in their factories around town. They may even wash dishes in a restaurant like this. But mingling amongst the 'Chosen People' was enough to bring their self-indulgent, self-centered lives to a screeching halt. The men feeling an inexplicable resentment growing in their bellies. The women were flush with embarrassment from the fire growing in their loins. Both feelings wanting to be expressed, yet both having to be concealed in order to maintain some unwritten southern code of conduct.

The four men enjoyed the spotlight. Sipping on Bacardi and washing it down with frosty mugs of Blue Moon Ale, they took turns matching stares with the snobby businessmen and stoaking the coals of desire in the delicate Southern Belles. Their name was called over the intercom. They paid their tab, tipping the bartender heavily and telling him to remember them. They would surely be back. Free entertainment. This could very well be their meeting place to discuss the progress of their plans.

Dinner began with four bowls of white chicken chili. A local favorite. Two orders of Shrimp Calhoun followed. Four skewers of grilled shrimp basted with Calhoun's own barbeque sauce. After another round of beer, this time Newcastle Nut Brown Ale, came four Caesar salads. Fresh and crisp, the men devoured the Caesars just as the main course arrived.

The group's server, Ashley, was given the challenge to bring the very best entrees that Calhoun's had to offer. In her opinion, she was equal to the task. Miguel was given the Steak Calhoun. A fourteen ounce top sirloin grilled to medium-rare perfection. As was the case with their shrimp appetizer, the sirloin was basted with barbeque sauce while grilling. Garlic mashed potatoes was the starch. All four were given the same vegetable, Spinach Maria. This was a house specialty. A delicate blend of spinach, cheese, crushed red pepper and some spices they just couldn't put their fingers on. They all agreed, however, that this was fantastic.

Sandoval was treated to a full rack of baby back ribs. Ribs that have won several awards across Tennessee, as well as the entire country. A heaping portion of seasoned curly fries accompanied his entrée. The ribs were tender and delicious. Ashley's second choice was rewarded with a pile of bones sucked entirely clean.

Javier was pleased with his selection as well. A half chicken grilled to perfection, also basted with Calhoun's famous barbeque. The skin had just the right crispness and smoky flavor without the slightest bit of over-charring. The Smokey Mountain Baked Beans were just the right combination of spicy and sweet. There surely must have been some molasses involved in their preparation.

Lastly, a beautiful blackened salmon was waiting for Troncillo's approval. Spicy, moist and not overly pungent. Another hit for Ashley. Accompanied by a twice-smashed potato, the meal was delectable. Tranquillo had no problem clearing his plate.

The men opted for snifters of Gran Marnier for their dessert. There was no room left for anymore food. Their bill came to just under two hundred dollars. They left Ashley a fifty percent tip, along with Sandoval's phone number. He and Ashley had been quite flirtatious with one another all evening long. She thanked the group with a dazzling smile and a stereotypical 'Y'all come back now...ya hear!' Sandoval was given a wink and a semi-coy, semi-mischievous smile. He had truly made an impression.

The gentlemen finished their after dinner drinks and headed toward the door. It was 10:30pm. A warm breeze drifting off the Tennessee River rounded out what was, thus far, a most pleasant evening.

The feast had been a success. Now it was time to get wild. The crew hopped in the Escalade and headed west on I-40. They were off to find pleasure at The Katch One.

Chapter 16

Samantha Sullivan sat in the dingy hole they called a dressing room. It was almost time to go on stage. The first show each night was always the toughest.

Without modern chemistry she would never have been able to do it. Cut out on a mirror in front of her were three large lines of cocaine. She put the razor in her little, black-lacquer jewelry box that held her earrings. Sam picked up a sterling silver straw that had been given to her by one of the girls that quit this madness for a better life. Starting from the left, she began to snort the little mountain ranges of inspiration. Anesthesia? No… inspiration. After the third line slid effortlessly up through the straw, Sam's head tilted back. She dropped the straw on the mirror as the rush of coke brought on the desired euphoric state.

The transformation had begun. As the numbness in her nose spread throughout her body, Sam could feel her man-made courage rising. She looked toward her costume rack to pick out her identity for the night. Who did she want to be tonight? The answer to that was anyone but herself. She couldn't face those hungry eyes, wandering hands and pathetic come-ons as Samantha. She needed a buffer.

"Lulu Belle," she blurted out as she reached for her imitation Dallas Cowboy's cheerleader's outfit. White spandex trimmed in metallic blue sparkles. Underneath her bikini top were twin red, white and blue stars pasted over her nipples. The outfit was so tight it amazed her that she could slip into it without a shoehorn. The thought of that made her laugh outloud.

She heard her song blasting out of the speakers in the showroom. That was her cue. They were waiting for her now. Waiting to throw their hard earned money at her. Slipping bills into the blue silk band wrapped around her upper thigh. Money that their wives were expecting to pay the mortgage or phone bill. They didn't seem to care. A roof over their wife and kids heads played second fiddle to their own lustful pursuits.

"All right gentlemen. Here comes the spotlight girl of the evening. Please…let's give a big round of applause for our favorite little pom-pom girl…Lulu Belle!"

Samantha picked up the bottle of Jameson's Irish Whiskey she kept on her vanity. She raised it to her lips and took three long pulls of the brown nectar. She wiped her mouth with her forearm and headed out to the stage. Praying to God to get her through another night of the humiliation and degradation that seemingly rid her of her values and caused her life to become such a dirty secret.

Chapter 17

Troncillo filled up four large vials of cocaine as the Escalade came to rest in the unpaved, hole-filled excuse for a parking lot surrounding the Katch One strip club. They believed that the cocaine assured them of special treatment wherever they went. This was especially true at strip clubs. At least that's the way it was throughout South Florida. The everyday average Joe was stuffing hundreds of dollars in the girl's G-strings hoping for a chance to cop a feel. If they were lucky, and spent enough money, one of the girls might grind them enough during a lap dance to get them off. Then they would sit in their cum-drenched boxers with a glazed look over their eyes and a stupid grin on their face. To look at them, you'd think they just won Lotto.

Miguel used to laugh at those poor souls. They didn't have a clue. He wasn't about to let them in on his secret. Escobar had never left a strip joint without sampling the wares of several of the girls. That's what the coke was for. Money got you in the door, but the cocaine was the 'panty dropper.' It released any remaining inhibitions the girls had. A couple good blasts in the Champagne Room and the girls would let their hair down.

Javier peeled off four crisp twenty dollar bills and slid them through the opening of the bullet-proof window that housed the club's cashier. The four men paraded through the club unnoticed. The pathetic patrons were oblivious to anything that didn't involve tits jiggling or some bimbo sliding up and down a pole.

The group settled into a corner booth to the left of the stage. They had barely gotten themselves seated when a short, busty brunette sauntered up to the table. She was scantily clad in a bright orange thong and pasties bearing the University of Tennessee logo. She introduced herself as Tiffany and said she was their hostess for the evening. Apparently hostess was more dignified than waitress. Sandoval asked her to recommend a good bourbon. Her recommendation was Maker's Mark and Sandoval urged her to bring back a bottle. She remarked that it was club policy to serve drinks by the glass. This policy must not have been etched in stone. All it took was Tiffany staring into the eyes of Benjamin Franklin. Moment's later, Tiffany returned with the bottle of Maker's Mark and four rocks glasses filled with ice.

Samantha's eyes locked on the four nicely dressed Latinos entering the club. They were like shiny gemstones amidst a sea of coal. Sam immediately saw dollar signs. Rent. Cable. Two of the men had been here before and the payoff was huge. She walked out of The Katch with eight hundrd dollars, a free night of partying and a nice stash to take home to give her a jumpstart the next day. In all honesty, however, Sam's 'free' night of partying had been anything but free. She could still picture the one called Troncillo with his hands digging into her hips, slamming his manhood into her from behind. First vaginally, then anally. All the while, Javier holding her by her hair, forcing her to please him with her mouth. Both men invaded her with a ferocious tenacity unlike anything she had ever experienced before. Nowhere to run. Knowing all to well that she was in it until both men had their way with her. Sam thought to herself how amazing it was how this life she was living had altered her definition of free.

Javier motioned to Samantha as she descended the stairs to the left of the main stage. She gave him her million dollar smile and held up a finger as if to say one minute. The entourage sat laughing and telling stories while they made their assault on the bottle of Maker's Mark. None of the participants knowing that this was the beginning of something that would be unforgettable for some and absolutely regrettable for one.

Chapter 18

Frank James stood alone in the empty parking lot that he hoped would soon be full of faithful patrons eager to fill their bellies at the Knuckle Sandwich Deli. Amidst the backdrop of the occasional car passing by, Frank stood in awe at the fact that what he had worked so hard for was finally coming to fruition. The excitement and anticipation of turning this empty space into a thriving eatery was all he could stand. That was what had him standing out here at three in the morning. Sleep had eluded him. His was mind unable to rest until the first coat of paint hit the walls, the signage was hung out front and the staff had been carefully selected and trained. First things first. All that would come in time.

That's what his fellowship had drilled into him from the start. Easy does it. Keep it simple. All of these catch phrases began to invade his thoughts. He had found that when he followed these principles, everything seemed to fall into place.

Tonight would be no different. He picked up the five gallon bucket of paint that he had gotten yesterday at Home Depot. He dug for the keys in his pocket as he strode toward the glass door that stood between him and his destiny. He retrieved the keys and opened the door to his future.

After several trips to the Concorde, Frank was ready to get to work. He had a long day ahead of him. His first task was to fix several holes that were scattered throughout the walls of his domain. Grabbing his putty knife and spackle, he went to work. With three hours left until sunrise and his CD player pumping out old Van

Halen tunes, James could get a big jump on the day's work.

At six-thirty, with all the holes patched and sanded, Frank decided to take a break. He hopped in his car and jetted down to the Perkins out in West Knoxville. He settled in and ordered his usual breakfast. Steak and eggs, home fries and a side of grits. James washed it down with a large Coke. He never had a cup of coffee in his life, so Coke became his source of caffeine. It wasn't uncommon for him to have a twelve pack or more each day.

With a full stomach and some renewed inspiration, Frank headed east on Kingston Pike. He had a few stops to make. First, he would hit the Wal-Mart on Walker Springs Road. He decided to get his office supplies there instead of Office Max. For some reason, he had a soft spot for Wal-Mart. Next, he pulled into Kinko's, where he picked up the copies of the application for employment that he had drawn up himself. With a quick stop at the West Hills Sign Shop, he was on his way back to the deli.

West Knoxville was in full swing by now. Kingston Pike was packed in both directions. I-40 East was already backing up as both students and businessmen alike headed into the heart of the city's business district and the UT campus. Frank saw dollar signs in the windshield of each vehicle on the road. One part of the business he hoped to build was the breakfast trade. The traffic boosted his enthusiasm to another level. He could feel himself wanting to jump out and hit the ground running even before his Chrysler was fully stopped in the parking space.

In an instant, Frank had his car unloaded, the step ladder out and the 'OPENING SOON' banner ready to be hung. He wanted people to be aware way ahead of time that there would be a new deli opening in the near future. He welcomed and took time out for anyone who stopped by to see the progress or ask any questions about the menu, the atmosphere or even about Frank himself.

Chapter 19

"So, where are you guys from?" Samantha was curious to find out more about her new found benefactors.

The men all looked at Miguel to answer the question. They were unsure of just how much information they should offer.

"We're from Florida. North Miami, actually."

"Why in the hell would you want to come to Tennessee? There ain't shit up here. I'd give anything to be by the beach."

"We don't plan on staying too long. Believe me. We just came up here to see a friend of ours that moved here from Pompano Beach. We haven't seen him in about three years. We figured we'd come up and surprise him."

"That's so cool! I bet he'll be psyched. Do you know where he lives or works or anything?"

Miguel was interested in seeing where this would go. Knowing full well where to locate Frank James, he decided to pretend not to. He would throw out some bait. The odds of this silly girl knowing James was close to zero. But... what if she did? What if he could get some valuable information that would help make his dream come true?

"Not really. I mean, we know he lives right around Knoxville, but other than that we have to play it by ear. We didn't want to call him and ruin the surprise. We figured, how big could this place be?"

Samantha was starting to get confused. "That seems kinda weird. That's a long way to come without being sure you'll find your friend."

Miguel laughed, "We had some spare time. Besides, we needed a vacation. Why not Tennessee?"

"Whatever! Where are we going, anyway? Do we have time to stop off for last call? I know a great place. It's called Spicy's."

JACKPOT!

"Spicy's?" Sandoval looked at Miguel and grinned. "That's where our friend used to work. Maybe you know him? Frank James."

"You're shittin' me! Do I know him? I used to sleep with him. We were just friends... with benefits. He used to close Spicy's and we'd get high as hell. He don't work there anymore. We don't see each other much because he's been clean for a few years now. It makes it awkward. I don't want to quit and he can't be around it."

Miguel couldn't have been happier. He grabbed Samantha by the hand. As he raised her hand to his lips, he looked her right in the eyes and said, "We won't be going to Spicy's tonight. You and I have much more important things to do. Besides, we have everything we need right here."

With that, he dumped a large pile of coke on the back of Sam's hand. He leaned down and took half the pile with a quick sniff. After he closed his eyes and shook his head, Miguel motioned to Sam to finish the pile. She gladly accepted. Once the cocaine was gone, Miguel kissed her hand and then her lips. Softly at first. Then with a fierce hunger.

Miguel placed his palm along side Sam's face. She leaned into the heat from his hand. In an instant, his gaze went from one having romantic undertones to one with a purpose.

"We have all night to enjoy each other's company. I'm looking forward to that very much. You have no idea just how much. But first, I want you to tell me everything you know about Frank James, his family and his friends."

At that moment, Samantha believed that God would answer her prayers on this night. She would not live to see tomorrow. She would never have to dance again. There was no fear. No panic. The only feeling she had was that of a tragic waste of life. Not loss... just waste.

Chapter 20

Frank's plan seemed to be working. He had already gotten four or five people to stop in and ask what it was that would be opening soon. He took time with each of them, asking their names, introducing himself as the owner, explaining the menu and giving them a tentative opening date. This was what Frank was made for. He always made people feel welcome. Even special. He never underestimated the value of a good first impression. It was essential to him. Word of mouth could be the best, or worst, type of advertisement for any business. A bad first impression had ruined many a business venture before it even had a chance to get rolling. That was not going to happen to the Knuckle Sandwich Deli if he had anything to do with it.

It was just before lunch when Frank had finished organizing his office. The last piece had just been delivered by the guys from the Brown Squirrel. It was a cherry computer desk that had just the right space for his computer and it's accessories. He had seen it months ago while shopping for a bed for his niece Rachel. James fell in love with it. He paid cash and the salesman assured him that he could have it delivered whenever he was ready for it.

Frank had built three shelves of matching cherry and mounted them on the wall adjacent to the desk. These would be home for his training manuals, nightly sales report binders, manager's log and countless other items he would need access to on a daily basis.

His phones, fax and computer were all in place awaiting the

technicians from Southern Bell to hook them up. They were scheduled to be here on the twenty-seventh of May at nine in the morning. Once they were activated, this project would really be in full swing. As it was now, Frank had to leave the building frequently to get things done. Mostly because of materials that had to be copied or laminated and designs that needed finishing touches. Even though he was able to communicate by cell phone, these other things had to be hand delivered without the convenience of the fax machine. Each trip away from the building meant something at the deli was not getting the attention it deserved.

The locksmith had just left after installing the office safe. It was a newer model that required both a combination and a key. The heavy black eyesore was encased in a wooden cabinet that matched the rest of the décor.

Now that the office was done, Frank could concentrate on transforming this empty shell into his dream. He broke out the drop cloths and spread them out, covering the entire floor. He would need to put a coat of primer on the walls first. Eventually, the walls would be covered with a dark, soothing forest green. James had considered using a rich maroon color on the walls, but that thought was short lived. Maroon was associated with the Alabama Crimson Tide. Tennessee's arch nemesis. The people in Knoxville would have burned down the deli rather than eat in it if it reminded them of their most hated rival.

Frank walked over to the CD player he brought to keep him company. Looking over the collection of disks he had with him, he decided on Sirsy. Sirsy was a local band that Frank got turned on to when he spent a summer working in Lake George, New York. He became friends with the singer and had purchased three of their CD's. As he looked at the CD cover, he noticed that this one was the Melanie had autographed. "To a great chef and greater friend", Frank read aloud. He wondered how the band was doing these days.

With the bluesy melodies bringing back sweet memories, Frank grabbed his brush and ladder and began the renovation of his lifelong dream. Lunch could wait. He attacked his work with the enthusiasm of a teenage boy trying to become a man on prom night. Life was good. Everything inside him told him that the best was yet to come. He seemed to have finally turned the corner in his life where it was no longer ruled by chaos and despair.

Chapter 21

Detective Benny Robbins of the Knox County Sheriff's Department was a miserable son-of-a-bitch. At five feet nine inches tall, two hundred sixty-five pounds, he was the farthest thing from being a poster boy for any police department. His head was shaped like a giant melon. With a large hook nose, flapping jowles, beady little eyes and a unibrow, it was easy to see why his dance card was never full. His slovenly looks were combined with the personality of a yeast infection. His polyester pants and short sleeve button-down oxfords with sweat stains under the armpits completed this most undesireable package.

Robbins' career was a tribute to the old adage, 'It's not what you know, but rather who you know'. While he had worked for Knox County for twenty three years, the first nineteen of them were spent in the correction's division. It wasn't until his cousin, Tim Sanders, was elected Knox County Sheriff, that Robbins was set free from the jails. His meteoric rise to homicide detective had left a bad taste in the mouths of his fellow officers. In many cases, years of hard work and dedicated service were passed over by an obvious case of nepotism.

It was Robbins who was first to arrive at the scene. That made him lead detective on this one, much to the chagrin of the patrolmen who had secured the crime scene. He pulled his Crown Victoria to a stop on Central Avenue in front of Patrick Sullivan's, one of the popular eateries in Knoxville's trendy Old City. The blue lights from the throngs of patrol cars barricading off a two block strip of Central cast an eerie glow throughout the Old City. With sunrise maybe a half an hour away, Robbins slammed the door to his Crown Vic and strode toward the crime scene.

The girl's body was found by the cleaning crew hired to clean Lucille's, another popular restaurant in the heart of the Old City. The cleaners consisted of an Hispanic couple, Luis and Anna Munoz, and their daughter Teresa. Luis had raced from inside when he heard the shriek of his daughter out back near the dumpster. Teresa stood frozen with horror, her eyes locked on the blood-stained leg hanging out of the dumpster. Munoz put his powerful arms around his daughter and led her back inside. He dialed 911 as his wife reassured Teresa that everything would be alright.

There were two Knoxville City cops guarding the dumpster. Robbins approached them with his usual sarcasm and ignorance. "Why do they always gotta die so fuckin' early in the morning?"

"This one's pretty bad, sir," the tight-lipped patrolman responded, trying with all his might to hold in his contempt for this hard hearted bastard.

"Yeah! Yeah! Let me take a look."

Robbins approached the stiff with his 'You've seen one, you've seen 'em all' mentality. As he peered over the edge of the dumpster, he gasped. He swallowed hard to keep the bile from coming up. He turned, wide-eyed, toward the two patrolmen. He couldn't speak. They saw the horror in his eyes.

"We found her purse lying right beside her. Her name is Samantha Sullivan. There was eight hundred dollars and a couple of grams of coke in there as well. That pretty much rules out robbery on this one. Whoever did this is one sick son-of-a-bitch."

Robbins turned his attention back to the corpse. He thought he had seen it all. He was wrong. The girl was propped up against several bags of trash. One leg hanging over the side of the dumpster with the other leg spread to her left. She was bare naked. Her arms bent at the elbows. Her severed head lay in her hands. Eyes and mouth wide open. No doubt expressing the terror she saw coming.

Robbins took a deep breath, turned away from the girl and tried to give some commands to the City boys without having his voice crack. "Clear a path for the Coroner's van. Whatever you do, keep those fucking news cameras far away from this shit. One shot of this on the front page and this whole friggin' town will be in hysterics."

This was no fly by night act of violence. Something like this required a goal. A real sense of purpose. What that purpose was, Robbins had no earthly idea. He was sure, however, that this city was about to be exposed to a horror the likes it had never seen.

Chapter 22

Frank stood with his hands on his hips as he marveled at his work. In less than twenty four hours, this barren tomb at the end of Montvale Shopping Square had already begun to come to life. Dingy, faded walls rejuvenated with new hope that came in the form of a fresh coat of paint. He couldn't help but think, as did the owners of this particularly unprofitable strip mall, that this deli was just the right thing to attract other businesses to Montvale and turn this lemon into the thriving center of commerce it once was.

He visualized the exact location of the three large deli coolers he expected to arrive tomorrow from Central Restaurant Supply. The rest of the décor would be easy, once the coolers were up and running. Fortunately for James, his lease included a fully functional kitchen, complete with a large walk-in cooler and freezer, flat top grill, a broiler and three deep fryers, all of which were in good working order. There was already a hood in place, as well as an Ansul system to satisfy the Fire Marshall. Best of all, his landlord had already sent in a cleaning crew to get the kitchen looking like new. That was a nasty job that James was blessed to have avoided.

James figured it was time to hang his 'NOW HIRING ALL POSITIONS" sign. His interviews would be informal to say the least. It would probably be three days before the dining room tables, chairs and booths would arrive. He believed in standing tall and looking them straight in their eyes anyway. The ones that were fidgety and uncomfortable probably weren't keepers. He was looking for employees that were 'people' people. Confident in any environment, with the ability to look Frank in the eyes and let him know why it would be to his advantage to hire this particular person. And…he liked them hungry. Hungry for money, for hours and for a chance to advance.

God knows he'd get his share of mama's boys and sorority girls with a silver spoon in their mouths. But there were always one or two diamonds in the rough.

Willing to learn, eager to grow. That's what he was looking for. Someone he could trust when he wasn't around. Someone that would do the next right thing even when no one was looking. That's how James was when he first hit the workforce. Even though he had recently struggled, that's how he was once again.

Frank broke out some boxes filled with decorations. Pictures and boxing memorabilia that would give the Knuckle Sandwich Deli it's character. Boxing gloves, robes and autographed photos of the sport's greatest legends would provide idle chit chat for some and perhaps a stroll down memory lane for others. They would also help to keep children occupied so that their parents could get some well deserved peace and quiet, as well as a chance at eating a full meal without too many emergencies. There would even be a miniature boxing ring where patrons could imagine themselves settling the score with an old boss or maybe a know-it-all neighbor.

James began organizing his memorabilia, waiting for potential employees and inquisitive patrons-to-be, along with the beer representatives he was expecting from both Eagle and Cherokee Distributors. It had been a very productive day thus far. Full of energy, regardless of the fact that his day had started well before dawn. There would be plenty more of these days ahead. That was the nature of the beast. Restaurant life. Hectic to say the least, but Frank wouldn't have it any other way. At least this time he was doing all this for himself instead of some nameless, faceless corporation. This time he could enjoy and benefit from the fruits of his labor.

Chapter 23

Benny Robbins sat at his desk at the City County Building, overlooking the Tennessee River. Exhausted from canvassing the Old City, looking for for anyone that had seen suspicious activity late last night or early this morning. He questioned business owners and residents alike. His blanket coverage began in the heart of the Old City and swept out to cover Jackson Avenue, State Street, Depot Avenue and Summit Hill Drive. Nothing! He had sent a few uniformed Sheriff patrols to cover South Gay Street. Specifically, the Rescue Mission on the corner of South Gay and Jackson. Knoxville City Officers were canvassing Magnolia.

The longer he went without any leads, the less likely this case was to be solved. Law enforcement agencies generally used forty eight hours as a guideline to whether or not they will be successful on any given case. They believe the trail cools off considerably after this time period. Robbins found this to be true.

Having heard nothing from his fellow Sheriff Deputies or the Knoxville City Police, Robbins decided to get caught up on his paperwork. His superiors would want to be kept up to date on this one. His mind wandered. Deep inside he feared that this was not an isolated incident. It wouldn't be long before bodies started stacking up. Robbins sat typing at his desk when his phone erupted throughout the squad room.

"Robbins, Homicide."

"Benny? Bert Benson down here at CIU." CIU was short for the Criminal Investigations Unit. They were the guys that covered every inch of the crime scenes. Photos, fingerprints, etcetera.

"Whadda you got for me, Bert?"

"We couldn't come up with a single print that didn't belong to Sullivan, the cleaning girl or people that work at Lucille's. The body is at the Coroner's office now. Bucky Gordon is handling it personally."

"Can't you freakin' guys call with good news once in a while?"

"Well, actually, there may be something you want to check out. We found her little black book in her purse. As I went through, I noticed that the J's were torn out."

"Big fuckin' deal! Maybe the bimbo didn't know anybody that started with a J?"

"That's what I thought …at first."

"Are you gonna make me guess for Christ's sake?"

"Who shit in your Corn Flakes this morning, Benny? Anyway, we located her cell phone in the bottom of the dumpster. We checked the last call that was made from the phone trying to get an idea of the actual time of death. Turns out it was made at three thirty in the morning and lasted forty five minutes. I'm betting Bucky places the time of death around three thirty."

Robbins sat quietly for a moment. It seemed strange that the call lasted that long. He wasn't sure why, it just seemed strange. If Benson was right, then there was a possibility that the killer got to Sullivan while she was on the phone. That meant that somewhere there could be a cell phone out there with a message on it that contained the details of the slaying. It was a long shot, but hell, he didn't have anything else to cling on to for hope.

"Good job Bert. Who was the pigeon she made her last call to?"

"That's were it really gets interesting. She called an old friend of yours… Frank James."

"Well I'll be a son-of-a-bitch! This just got really juicy. Thanks Bert."

Frank James. Robbins cringed at the thought of him. James caused trouble for years and had virtually gotten a get out of jail free card because he cooperated on a drug sting operation that encompassed three states.

The FBI got involved. Robbins would never forget the day Agent Sandy Borden told him that he was taking over the case. How he hated that bleeding-heart liberal bastard. After James helped bring down the largest dope ring the southeast had ever seen, Borden decided to drop all charges against James. Robbins' fists clenched at the thought of that atrocity. Borden felt James should be given the chance to be rehabilitated rather than incarcerated. Robbins felt he should fry.

That was old news. Robbins began to salivate. There would be no intervention on this one. James was his. He would implicate him even if he had to falsify evidence. What started out to be a cloudy day for Benny Robbins had just revealed it's silver lining.

Chapter 24

James flipped open his cell phone to call his sister Rose. She was going to help hang the boxing memorabilia today. One missed call flashed across the monitor. Frank hit the view button to see who called. Samantha. That was weird. He hadn't heard from Sam for a while now. Ever since he tried to get her to stop stripping. The call was made at three thirty in the morning. She must have been high as hell. Oh well. He figured she would be passed out for a while, so he'd call her later.

James dialed Rose.

"Hello?"

"Hey, I can't believe you're up. Are you still gonna help me today?"

"Yeah. I'll help. Are you okay?"

"Why wouldn't I be? Everything's going just the way it should."

There was a silence. "You haven't been watching the television, have you?"

"No. Why?"

"There was a murder in the Old City last night. The body was found in the dumpster behind Lucille's. They're not saying much, but supposedly it was pretty gruesome."

"There's a bunch of freaks down there Rose. You know how many lunatics I personally have kicked out of Spicy's in my day. It's a shame, but life goes on. I'll be right over to get you."

"Frank. I don't think you understand."

"What? What don't I understand? People die. It was only a

matter of time before it happened in the Old City. What makes this murder different from what happens everywhere else?"

Rose felt a lump in her throat. She didn't quite know how to tell her brother exactly who's body was found. She knew she didn't want him to find out from anyone else. Someone that didn't understand the connection. She decided on the direct approach.

"Frank… it was Samantha. Samantha Sullivan."

That hit Frank hard. He could feel the air seeping out of his body. He couldn't breathe. It was as though he took a Mike Tyson right hand to the solar plexus. He dropped on the couch. Tears welled up in his eyes.

Thoughts and emotions swirled through his brain. *How? Why? I should have made her quit!* Frank dropped the phone and raced to the kitchen sink, vomiting. His entire body heaving.

Rose waited on the line. She heard her brother getting sick. She had to be there for him today. She prayed silently that this wouldn't be too much for him to handle. This would surely test his resolve to stay clean and sober.

Chapter 25

Miguel Escobar and his posse sat in their room at the Hampton Inn watching the commotion on television that was caused by their handiwork. A grin pasted across his face as the first step in his plot for revenge was complete.

This step was actually a bonus. What were the chances of meeting a stripper that was in tight with his prey? When the police found her phone with Frank James' number the last one called, they would surely hassle him. Nothing too serious at first. Just enough to disrupt his comfortable little life. Perhaps hinder his ability to focus. With other matters pending, he might just need someone he could trust to help him run his deli.

Escobar would be that person. He already had his fake identity. His plan… to infiltrate the enemy camp. He would gain the trust of his most hated foe. He would get to know intimate details of James' life. His desires, his loves, his friends, his past and his family. He would use anything and everything to destroy James' life. Lots of pain and suffering. And, ultimately, death.

Each of his men were given their roles to play in this drama. They had gone over it time and time again to be sure there would be no mistakes. Each man knowing that there life was on the line if they slipped up.

Chapter 26

Tires squealed as James flew into his sister's driveway. He had to talk to her. He had to try and make some sense of this situation. Once he regained his composure at his house, the reality of the situation came crashing down on James with the force of Niagara Falls. *The phone call. What was it all about? Why did she try to call me?* He would check his messages as soon as he got inside.

Frank slammed the front door and was immediately attacked by Zeus, his sister's Golden Lab. He loved that dog, but now was not a good time. He gave Zeus a quick smooch and scratch at the base of his back. That caused Zeus to drop and roll every time, providing enough time to escape into Rose's room.

She came out of the bathroom with a look of worry and concern that James hadn't been subjected to in three years. His family didn't have to worry as long as he stayed clean.

"Frank! You scared the hell out of me. What's going on?"

"I'm not sure, but we're about to find out together." James dialed his voicemail and put it on speaker phone.

"... Help! I'm in trouble! I think he's going to kill me. Frank...noooo..." Samantha's voice was cut off. What followed sent chills through both Frank and Rose. It was unbelievable. High-pitched shrills. The sound of something hard was crashing into what must have been flesh and bone. Samantha sobbing. Begging. Pleading to know why this was happening to her.

Frank jumped off the bed. "What's that?" A motor erupted in the background. The killer revved the engine. "Oh my God!" Could that be what Frank thought it was? "Not a fucking chiansaw!"

Samantha let out one last scream and then… silence. It was over. Frank and Rose staring at each other, mouths agape. They had the murder on tape.

They sat in silence, amazed at what had just transpired. Before James could say anything, a face appeared on the television screen. A familiar face. A definitely not-so-friendly face. This face could change Frank's life forever.

Benny Robbins, Homicide Detective for the Knox Count Sheriff's Department, was talking about the murder. He said they had recently gotten a lead that they would check out as soon as the autopsy was completed.

"Yeah they got a lead. They found her phone. Guess who was the last person she called. I bet Robbins' pecker is hard thinking about how he's going to connect me with this shit."

Rose understood immediately. Robbins would come gunning for her brother. "You've got to beat him to the punch. Get your lawyer and get your ass down to the Sheriff's Department. Make them see you have nothing to hide. That you've come to help."

Frank sighed. He knew she was right. That fact didn't seem to make this any easier, though.

"Alright. I'll drop you off at the deli and I'll head downtown. I can't get behind down there. I need you to get those walls decorated. There's also a couple of shipments due today. Just check the invoices carefully and I'll deal with them when I get back."

"No problem, brother. Don't worry about a thing." Rose had a plan.

Chapter 27

"Hey Robbins! They need you downstairs."

"I could give two shits! I'm busy here!"

Deputy Coulter smiled. He couldn't wait to see how this played out. "I really think you'll want to be going down there. Trust me."

"How the fuck do you know what I want and don't want?"

"Just trust me on this one."

Robbins hopped on the elevator and pressed 'L'. When the doors opened up in the lobby, Robbins just about shit himself. He took a deep breath and walked over to the two men standing by the receptionist's desk. "Well, well, well! I'll be a son-of-a-gun. Look what the cat dragged in?"

James approached Robbins. There would be no handshakes or other pleasantries. These men loathed each other with a passion. No need for politeness. James looked at his lawyer, Brad Covington. Covington gave him a nod and James stuck out his hand.

"I've got something I'm sure you'll want to hear." He handed over his cell phone. "This has to do with your lead, no doubt."

"You're turnin' yourself in? How sweet." Robbins grinned, keeping his beady eyes in direct contact with James'.

"Look, I don't know if this will help you out or not. I noticed the call this morning. Listen to the message. I caught Samantha Sullivan's murder on tape. It's pretty sick."

"Why did she call you, pretty boy? Did she need some good drugs?" Robbins was trying to get a rise out of Frank. He loved that his position allowed him to get away with it.

"I have no idea why she called. I haven't talked to her in months."

"Pretty big coincidence that she called you right before she was whacked. Maybe she was callin' for help. Or maybe, just maybe, she was callin' to give us a clue as to who was trying to kill her. What happened, Frank? She wouldn't give up the pussy and you got mad?"

Frank's pulse quickened. Rage was building in his heart. He began to lurch after Robbins. Covington grabbed Frank's arm to hold him back. This type of reaction was just what Robbins was fishing for.

"Look you miserable fuck…she was my friend. What gives you the right to stand here and desecrate her character. She was just murdered for God's sake.

Why don't you spend less time on the jokes and more time doing your job. Put down the donuts and find her killer you pathetic piece of shit!"

"Oh, I'll do my job. You can bank on it, boy. Do me a favor? Don't take any trips in the near future. I'm pretty sure we'll have some questions for you. I'd hate to have to come looking for you."

"You know where I am, weasel."

Robbins turned toward the elevator and started to enter when he glanced back at James and his attorney. "Frankie-boy… don't think for one minute that your coming to see me clears you from the suspect list. This whole thing wreaks of your foul stench. Y'all have a nice day."

Chapter 28

It was just past noon when James arrived back at the deli. He was twisted. This was definitely not what he needed right now. He needed to focus every bit of energy he had on getting this place open.

He got out of the Concorde and trudged over to the front door. Frank was blown away by what he saw. His troops had rallied around him. His sister must have gotten on the horn as soon as he dropped her off.

All his favorite people were there. Mark Length, Carl Metcalf... even the tattoo boys. There was even one face that Frank had never seen before. "This place looks unbelievable. Everything up on the walls and the tables and chairs assembled to boot."

Frank gave hugs all around until he got to the face that was unknown, yet not entirely unfamiliar. He couldn't quite figure out why. "And just who might you be?"

Rose stepped in. "He's an angel, that's who." She gave the newcomer a kiss on the cheek.

"My name is Marco. Marco Bellizi." He reached out his hand to Frank. "I came by to fill out an application. It looked like they needed some help. So... here I am."

Frank reached in his pocket and pulled out two twenty dollar bills. He tried to give them to his newfound volunteer.

"No, sir. That's not why I did this. I don't want your money. Well, I do... just not today."

The entire gang was looking at Frank. He stood there for a minute. *Could this guy be for real?* Finally, he smiled and shrugged his shoulders. "I guess that was your interview, kid. You're hired. You and I will sit down in a few and get to know each other and you can fill me in on what kind of skills you have. We'll talk money after that. See if we can come to an agreement that will be beneficial to us both."

Marco was beaming. He outwardly showed gratitude, while on the inside he felt nothing but contempt for this man. Behind his fake smile, his sick, twisted mind was going a mile a minute. *You fool! You have no idea that you are in for the ride of your life!*

Chapter 29

The next few hours consisted of finding just the right floor plan for the tables and booths James had ordered. Several different attempts. Several different failures.

At a quarter to three it was all over. Booths lined the west wall, four rows of three tables each filled in the rest. They kept the northeast corner vacant for the time being. That was where the boxing ring would go. Frank figured he could fit four tables comfortably inside the ring.

The last of the crew was leaving the Knuckle Sandwich Deli. Frank walked Johnny Tattoo out to his Harley. Marco watched with interest as the two men talked. There was no doubt they were very close. As Frank hugged the skinny, tattoo-covered man goodbye, the wheels in Marco's brain started working overtime. At that instant, he decided that Johnny Tattoo must die.

Frank returned to the deli and he and Marco sat in one of the booths. It was time to see what page young Marco was on. They had one order of General Tso's Chicken and an order of Spicy Noodles delivered from the Stir Fry Café. That was Frank's favorite spot.

Rose was keeping busy wiping down tables and booths and wall hangings. There wasn't much Frank couldn't say in front of her anyway.

"So, Marco, where are you from?"

"Well, I'm originally from Yonkers, New York. I know... I'm a Yankee. Is that going to be a problem?"

"I don't think so. I'm from New York ,too. Poughkeepsie. You know where that is?"

"Yeah. Upstate."

"What brings you south?"

"My parents moved us around a lot. New York, Pennsylvania, Jersey, Virginia, North and South Carolina. I guess the south just kinda stuck. When my folks moved to Miami, I decided to stay. That's when I moved to Knoxville."

"How long ago was that?"

"Six months. I met a girl. Thought I was in love. Well, I was… she wasn't. We got a place. Spent everything I had to get it set up. That's when it happened."

"What happened?"

"I went to pick her up at the chiropracter's office. Guess they forgot to lock the door. I walked in on her getting her back adjusted…vaginally!"

Frank saw the pain in Marco's eyes and decided not to push it. "Sorry I asked."

"It's okay. It's kinda funny when I say it out loud. Anyway, she got the apartment and I got drunk. I've managed to get by on odd jobs. Then I met this guy. He started talking to me about drinking. Said he used to go at it non-stop for weeks at a time. Said he lost everything. I acted like I didn't realize what he was talking about."

Marco's eyes shot down to his plate. His whole body sagged. "I knew he was talking about me. Trying to make me take a look at myself. Trying to give me hope. I've even been to a couple of those meetings." He paused and looked at Frank. "I don't even know why I'm telling you all this. It will probably change your mind about me."

Frank smiled. He remembered how hard it was when he started thinking about surrendering to his disease. Addicton was hell. Admitting it was even worse. It sure did take courage to tell someone. Especially someone you didn't know from Adam. *This kid's got potential.*

"Tell you what, my man. I appreciate and applaud your honesty. I'm not changing my mind. If anything, you just secured your future here with me."

"Really?"

"Listen. In a couple of weeks I'll be celebrating three years clean. I know what you're going through. Been there. Done that. I'd be happy to help you out if you're serious about quitting. But, I have to tell you that I cannot and will not have that shit interfere with my business. And believe me…I'll know."

Frank could see the appreciation in Marco's eyes. He could relate with how good it felt to finally have someone understand the pain. Someone willing to look at your potential, rather than judge you on your mistakes. He believed everyone deserved a second chance. He had gotten one. It was his turn to pass it on.

"Look, Marco. The past is just that… the past. You're starting here with a clean slate. It's up to you to fuck it up… or not."

"Thanks, Frank. I won't let you down."

"Don't let yourself down. You got a place to stay?"

"My car for now."

"I've got a spare room at my place. It's yours if you want it. When you get a few paychecks under your belt, we'll talk about rent. Your choice."

"Are you kiddin' me? I mean, yes sir. I would really appreciate it."

"Alright then. Follow me home tonight. I have to drop off Rose and then we'll get you settled."

"Frank? What's my job gonna be?"

"You're gonna learn the whole damn thing, my boy. We're going to see what you're made of."

Marco shook his head and laughed to himself. *This is going to be too easy!* Phase two was going better than he anticipated.

Chapter 30

Detective Robbins sat at his desk playing the tape of Samantha Sullivan's final message over and over again. He sat mortified at what he was hearing. What that poor girl must have gone through. Whoever did this was sick. Someone like this had no feelings of remorse. That's what worried Robbins so. Lack of remorse was a necessary quality of all budding serial killers. That was truly what he thought was at work here. This was no mugging or drug deal gone bad. This was pure hatred and evil.

Robbins wanted to pin this whole thing on James so badly he could taste it. He knew that this was hardly enough evidence to get the DA to make a move. On one hand, it sounded like Sullivan called James for help. That's probably how most people that listened to it would respond. This is where Robbins' personal prejudice against James came into play. He couldn't let go of the past. Wouldn't let go would be more precise. He lost all objectivity when it came to Frank James, but he didn't care. He was sure that he could live with any guilt that came from taking down his nemesis even if he was innocent. He knew that to suffer from guilt required a conscience. That was something he'd never been accused of having.

Still, that last thing she said gave him a glimmer of hope. "He's going to kill me... Frank... no." Was she identifying her assailant or was she crying out to the one person she actually thought could help?

Robbins decided to keep this bit of information under wraps for the time being. He needed to find someone that had insight on the relationship between James and Sullivan. Was there some sort of rift between them that would cause this catastrophe? If so, there were probably other parties involved.

Having held on to his original notion that this was no isolated incident, Robbins was sure there would be more mayhem to follow. If his hunch was correct, and it actually was James that was responsible for this, he was sure that James would slip up sooner or later. He couldn't imagine him being smart enough not to get caught. Then… he would pay dearly.

Robbins leaned back in his chair. With his eyes closed and a huge shit-eating grin exposing his nicotine-stained teeth, he drifted off to a happy place. The place where he got to inject the lethal doses of sodium pentothal, pancuronium bromide and potassium chloride. His own personal Nirvana. *Lights out Mr. James.*

Chapter 31

Home sweet home. It had been a long day for Frank. He had just dropped off Rose at home. He forced himself to pop in real quick to see his niece and nephew. The fact that he wanted Marco to meet them made his decision that much easier.

Marco passed the initiation with flying colors. The ultimate test being to gain acceptance from the king of the castle, Zeus. While the canine was tentative at first, he was soon on his back enjoying a full belly massage by Marco. He had made a new friend.

Frank and his new protégé rolled into the driveway of 205 Indiana Avenue. James had lived there since he arrived back from the halfway house in Nashville nearly two and a half years ago. It was a fairly old duplex in which Frank occupied the top apartment.

The two men climbed the stairs and entered the bachelor pad. Frank showed Marco his new room. The room was fully furnished, complete with cable television and a phone jack. Nothing fancy, but it beat the hell out of a 1990 Honda Accord.

After getting settled, Marco met up with his new roommate in the living room. Definitely a man's touch in here. The room revolved around a black leather sectional sofa and a forty four inch LG flat screen television that was perched upon an ultramodern black and silver glass entertainment center. One could easily see that James enjoyed his TV time. The entertainment center held a Bose surround sound system and a JVC DVD/VCR combo. All of the electronic accessories were black as well. Not wanting to immerse himself fully in the modern era was what prompted James to go with the

DVD/VCR combo. That and the fact that he loved his old VHS movies. Subconsciously, he thought as long as he could play his tapes, he wasn't getting too old. It is truly a harsh reality that everyone is, at one point or another, bitten by the vanity bug in some form. James was certainly no exception. His fear of getting old was due to the fact that he had wasted so much of his youth.

There was a large fireplace that was ensconced in marble. The sides were made up of two columns that looked as though they were designed to emulate the façade of many a southern plantation. The pearl colored mantle was home to what seemed like a shrine dedicated to Frank's recovery. He had kept all of the chips that were given to him by Alcoholics Anonymous that showed off his clean time.

There were also key chains representing the same thing from another fellowship that he was a part, Narcotics Anonymous. There were little plaques containing the twelve step program's slogans such as 'Easy Does It', 'Keep It Simple' and 'Just For Today.' The centerpiece of the shrine being an 8x10 picture of Frank and his sponsor, Carl Metcalf.

The rest of the room seemed to consist of nothing but bookshelves. Seemingly dozens of shelves that housed a multitude of books. Predominantly fictional novels, but there were many self-help and recovery type books as well. Reading became a passion of Frank's when he had to spend some time in the County Jail. Photos of Frank and his cronies were scattered throughout the many hard cover and paperback books.

Both men took up their positions on the sofa. Frank clicked on the news just as a nerdy little man was recapping the day's top story. Samantha Sullivan's murder. James cringed as the flood of emotions returned to him all at once. He was heartbroken over what had happened to Sam.

He had no answers or theories as to what happened to Samantha. There was nothing he could do to help or bring her back. The only thing James knew for sure was that he could not drink or drug over this horrible turn of events. That didn't stop those thoughts from invading his brain. Bombarding was more like it. They always did when something happened to cause him to be vulnerable. He would succomb to those thoughts at the drop of a hat in the past. He used drugs so he didn't have to feel the pain of the many tragedies that riddled his life. Of course, nine out of ten times, using the drugs would cause James to do something infinitely more painful than actually taking the time to grieve in the first place. That was the past. Today, he was a fighter. Today, he would stay clean to honor Sam's memory.

Marco liked the effects the death of Sullivan was having on James. He could actually feel his pain. He fed off it. Right then he decided that his posse should strike again quickly. Give James no time to recover. He wanted to kick James while he was down.

He excused himself from the living room by saying a shower was in order. Marco grabbed a change of clothes and his cell phone from his room. He locked the door, turned on the shower to cover his voice and dialed.

"Hola, *Jefe*. It is good to hear from you."

"Listen to me carefully. I want to strike again while the iron is hot. Have Javier and Troncillo take out target number two."

With that, Marco hung up the phone and looked to the Heavens. *This is all for you, Diego! All for you!*

Chapter 32

May 27, 2006

I t was business as usual at Spicy's. Every seat at the bar filled, pool tables packed and the CD jukebox blaring out familiar tunes. Kristy was tending bar. She was phenomenal. Having been voted sexiest bartender in Knoxville three years running, one might have expected her to exude a certain amount of self-love. Nothing could have been more to the contrary. She was down to earth, slightly innocent and remarkably coy.

She wasn't just eye candy for the patrons of Spicy's. Kristy commanded respect and controlled the atmosphere of the bar. She was held in high regards by both men and women alike. Anyone new to the bar learned quickly that abusive treatment and foul language were not tolerated by Kristy or anyone else who had any type of ties to this establishment.

Any person wishing to test the will of the management staff would do so only once. Many a degenerate had been expelled airborne through the heavy wooden doors that guarded this sanctuary. Mark Length and Frank James had made quite a name for themselves throughout the city as two men who could be your best friend or worst enemy.

On this particular evening, things were running smoothly. Kristy was at her jovial best. The bar crowd consisted of an amicable blend of regulars and first time customers. In the darkest corner of the bar, Johnny Tattoo was breaking out of his shell. Several triple-

72

screwdrivers and multiple shots of Irish Mist had removed any remaining inhibitions. He was in the middle of one of his best Robert Deniro impressions. These were usually reserved for the Tattoo Boys and staff of Spicy's. Tonight, however, Johnny was entertaining a couple of tourists. The two Hispanic men had won Johnny over instantly by buying the bar a round of shots. That's when they bellied up to the bar next to the half-sloshed man loaded with tattoos.

The more Johnny entertained, the more these men bought rounds. They were definitely Johnny's type of people. The man called Javi asked Johnny if there were anywhere safe to do a few bumps of cocaine. Johnny escorted the man to the employees bathroom. He had free rein of this place, but knew better than to take advantage of it. He let the man know that they couldn't make many trips back here without drawing suspicion.

Javier rewarded Johnny's kindness with a small vial of white powder. This way they would be able to make separate trips to the regular men's room.

They bonded well into the night. As the clock struck 3AM, the manager came out and informed everyone that it was time to leave. The two strangers told Johnny they would give him a ride home. Johnny was in no hurry. He was always one of the last men standing on any given night of partying.

The three men hopped into the black Cadillac Escalade and headed back to their hotel room. The party would go on. Or so Johnny thought.

As Johnny came to, he had to fight the urge to vomit. His head ached. His eyes had trouble focusing. When he did manage to collect himself, he realized that his hands and feet were bound tightly together with duct tape.

Confused and disoriented, Johnny looked at the two men staring at him from the front seat. "What are you two looking at? What's going on here?"

There was no response. The two men just smiled and continued looking at their prisoner.

"Oh! I get it! You two like boys. What's with the tape? A few hundred dollar bills would have been much more enticing. Definitely would have been more civilized."

Javier finally spoke. "We don't want to have sex with you

Johnny. We were sent here to kill you."

"Get the fuck outta here! Who put you up to this? Marcus? Daniel?"

"We have no idea who the hell you are talking about. We only know you, my friend."

Starting to realize that this might just be real, Johnny took a deep breath and said, "I didn't do anything to anybody. Why would someone send you to kill me?"

"This is true. You did no harm to anyone. The only thing you are guilty of is having Frank James as a friend."

The two men slipped gloves on and got out of the truck. They pulled Johnny out and sat him on the ground in the middle of a huge plastic tarp. After retrieving Johnny's phone from his pocket, Javier scrolled through his address book looking for James' number. He handed the phone to Johnny. It was ringing. *This all must be a sick joke*, Johnny thought.

"Frank… it's Johnny."

Javier snatched the phone away from him. At the same time, Troncillo pulled the rip cord and brought the chainsaw to life.

Johnny closed his eyes. "Ain't this a bitch!"

Those were Johnny's last words. His severed head bounced off the tarp several times before rolling to a stop. His body tilting to the left. Slowly at first. Finally picking up steam as though it were a tree crashing in the forest.

Chapter 33

May 28, 2006

Frank James laid in bed unable to decipher what just took place. Was he awake or was he dreaming? His dreams had become so vivid of late that he had trouble distinguishing between the two. As Frank glanced down at his hand, he realized he was clutching his Motorola Razor with all his might. The line was still open. There was an eerie silence. Frank called out but there was no answer.

James was positive he had heard his friend Johnny's voice. He called out once more. Nothing. Frank was about to hang up and chalk this bizarre occurance up to an active imagination when the horrendous, but familiar sound, corrupted the airways.

The revving of the chainsaw sent chills throughout Frank's entire body. Was this someone's idea of a cruel joke? No. This was no joke. Whoever was wielding the saw gave it one last rev and slid it through their target. There was a muffled gasp, followed by a freakish splitting of bone, and finally…silence.

The deed was done. Frank didn't move. He was petrified. The fear had immobilized him. What distressed him the most was the fact that he was totally helpless. The reality of the situation slowly creeped in. Frank broke out in a ghoulish sob. The thought of two people that were close to him dying in less than a week was more than he could handle.

Why these people? What was the connection? Frank had no answers to the questions forming in his brain. He only knew that people close to him were dying and calling him at the moment of their deaths. He was the only apparent common denominator. Who had he hurt so badly that would make them come after him like this? The possible answers to that question were too numerous to count.

James knew the body would be found. He was also willing to bet that the phone would be sitting out in the open at the scene for Detective Robbins. There would be hell to pay. Robbins would surely use these calls to get the District Attorney to go after James for murder.

This was absurd. Suddenly Frank was hit with an epiphany. He couldn't worry about Robbins right now. Someone was out there killing people that were significant to James, both past and present. He needed to make a list of people around him that were potential targets. He felt he was the only one who could put a stop to these senseless murders. He had to warn people of the potential danger they were in by merely being associated with him.

Chapter 34

James downed his second Coke of the morning while he sat on the living room sofa. One eye glued to CNN and the other to the paper on which he was making a list of those he felt were potentially in danger because of their connections with him. *How can I be sure to include everyone?* Frank went over the names that he came up with to this point.

Tina	Rose	Daniel	everyone in AA
Carl Metcalf	Tyler	Marcus	
Mark Length	Rachel	Melanie	

Frank realized that it would be almost impossible to think of everyone, let alone reach everyone. There were hundreds of potential victims in AA and NA alone. Even if he could reach them all, what would he say? They would think he was losing it. They might even think he relapsed and was having paranoid delusions. He might even start some kind of mass hysteria. That was no good. He would concentrate on those closest to him. That made sense.

His first plan of action was to call these people right away. But it was only four thirty in the morning. Frank decided to let them sleep until eight. No longer. He couldn't risk waiting because he had no idea when these sick bastards would strike again.

James looked up at the television screen. CNN was reporting on Samantha Sullivan's murder in Knoxville. While he didn't see how this particular murder was nationally prominent, he could understand why the Atlanta-based news program would show interest so soon. Atlanta was in the same region as Knoxville. A mere hundred fifty five miles south on I-75.

He feared they would have a follow-up segment by mid-morning. The killer would surely place Johnny's body somewhere to be discovered right away. It was just a matter of where and when it was found.

Frank was fighting with the idea of calling the police and telling them about his early morning call. There was no message this time. No proof of the call. If he didn't call, they might think he was hiding something. On the other hand, calling it in could possibly seem like he was trying to throw them off his scent. His brain was twisted. Paranoia definitely seemed to be setting in.

Common sense won out. Frank picked up the phone and dialed the Knox County Sheriff's Department. Detective Robbins wasn't in, so he explained who he was and why he was calling to the Sergeant on duty. The Sergeant listened earnestly and assured Frank that Robbins would get his message as soon as he showed up. He told Frank to be patient and Robbins would be in touch.

The rest of Frank's morning consisted of watching the news, slamming down Coca-cola's and figuring out how he could warn the people on his list without them thinking he was nuts or without creeping them out and causing chaos.

Escobar closed the bedroom door through which he had been listening. He enjoyed watching James struggle. His plan was working to perfection. The police would surely begin severely questioning James. Requesting an alibi. An alibi that could only be corroborated by Escobar himself.

With Frank's freedom in the balance, Escobar needed to remain focused as to the true nature of his plan. Escobar would indeed vouch for Frank. He needed him free to keep his plan in motion. The ultimate goal being James' death. Imprisonment was not a viable option.

Right now, Escobar needed to disguise his joy and go into the living room and show Frank some support. He needed to pry deeper into James' life in order to find his next victim. He was sure James would notify the people close to him here in Knoxville that they were in potential danger. They would have to cool it in this town for the time being.

It was time for some misdirection. There must be someone from another part of the country that had a sentimental attatchment with Mr. James. Escobar would peruse the pictures scattered throughout the house to find a suitable candidate. James wouldn't suspect a thing in his present condition. It would merely seem that his new roommate was interested in getting to know him better.

Miguel sat in his bed preparing himself for the role he would play in the next scene of the drama he was creating. He loved being the director. The puppet master. It gave him the power he craved by pulling other people's strings and pushing them in the direction he chose for them.

He took a deep breath and headed toward the living room. Consolation, provocation and manipulation would be his tools. Without realizing it, Frank would choose the next victim himself. *Irony,* Miguel thought. As he approached James he reminded himself to 'break a leg'.

Chapter 35

A thin ray of light peeped through a crack in the orange and brown polyester curtains that covered the cruddy windows of the fleabag motel. It was necessary to spend the night here. Certainly he could not have taken her to his real motel. To do that would mean he had to kill her and he was not prepared to do that just yet.

Sandoval pulled the covers back, exposing the supple, tan flesh of his tasty little morsel. He marveled at her body. It was close to perfect. Gravity had not started to have an effect on her. It helped that she was only twenty one. Her years of cheerleading helped to keep her in tip top shape. No body fat to speak of, yet she wasn't exactly anorexic either. Qiute voluptuous, in fact.

Sandoval had been thinking of her since she waited on them at Calhoun's.

She had played the shy, naïve type to a tee. Totally believeable, right up to the point where she sat him down on the bed and began her erotic striptease. Sandoval salivated just thinking about it. His manhood exploding to life. Perhaps he should wake her with another wild ride. Breakfast could wait. Actually, she would be the breakfast buffet.

A huge grin broke out across his face as he reminisced over last night's love-fest. Ashley was completely receptive to his every advance. He was amazed at the way she seemed to read his mind and anticipate his wants and needs.

With his loins ablaze, Sandoval prepared to mount his sleeping prey from behind. He hoped she would respond with the same enthusiastic bucking that she did last night. He truly enjoyed that. Apparently, so did she.

His attack was postponed, however, when his cell phone began blasting out Daddy Yankee's 'Rompe'. *Damn, Miguel. You can be such a pest!* "Hola, Jefe."

"Hello, my brother. I want you to get Javier and Troncillo ready to move. They are going to take a trip. I don't have much time before I go to work, so get them and meet me right away at the Waffle House on Alcoa Highway. I'll be there in twenty minutes."

Miguel's command was met with silence. As much as Sandoval wanted to tell him to get them himself, he couldn't. Miguel was the boss. Atleast for now he was. He would have to wait for another day to delight in Ashley's lusciousnesss.

"Is there a problem?", Miguel shouted. His irritation at having to wait for a response to his request rather obvious.

"No. No problem, Jefe. We'll be there in twenty minutes. Adios."

Sandoval sighed. He jotted down a few words on the pad of paper that sat by the phone. He tore off the page and placed it on the pillow. Trying not to wake her, he slipped on his shoes and quietly shut the door behind him. He truly hoped this disrespectful and hasty exit would not ruin his chances on another evening of pleasure with this sweet, young southern belle.

Chapter 36

Detective Benny Robbins was amazed at how little it took to ruin his day. He hadn't even signed in for the day when Sergeant Huggins delivered Frank James' message. He would have been pissed off getting any message at this point in the day. Getting one that mentioned James first thing in the morning had him completely incensed.

Robbins got to his cubicle, hung up his jacket and sat down ready to see exactly how James wished to screw up his world so early in the morning. His body became rigid at once. *Un...fucking...believeable.*

Even though his gut told him that it was just a matter of time before more atrocities were committed, the second one happened much quicker than he thought it would. An ominous prelude of things to come. What exactly was Frank James' connection to this whole stinking mess. Even Robbins wasn't naïve enough to think that James would willingly offer up information that could implicate him as the prime suspect of a murder investigation if he was, in fact, guilty. The reality of the situation, however, was that guilt or innocence was of no consequence to Robbins. He wanted to nail James' ass to a cross. Period!

Vigorously massaging his temples, Robbins had to force himself to stop focusing on his personal vendetta against James. At least for the time being. He also knew it would not be long before the shit hit the fan around the Department. He needed to have some answers for those higher-ups that would surely be riding his ass for results on this one.

Any time people were dying, especially in a loud, grotesque manner such as was the case here, there was no tolerance for failure. Patience was thrown out the window as well. If someone was unable to show significant progress on a case of this magnitude, they could be rest assured that their caseload would be tripled in the future. Their increased workload would not cosist of any glamorous cases either. It would be all the crap that nobody else wanted.

Robbins had just about used up his free passes that he acquired merely by being the Sheriff's cousin. While he had been fairly effective , solving the majority of cases sent his way, there had been two occasions in the past where he failed to come up with any leads or suspects. Consequently, those cases were abandoned without closure. In both instances, he was granted a reprieve by his high ranking cousin.

Any baseball fan knows…three strikes and you're out! The hammer would come down on him without question if he failed in his search with this much on the line. That fact may very well be the catylist for wanting James to be the patsy on this.

Robbins put out an all points bulletin on Johnny Tattoo. They needed to find him, alive or dead, before anyone else did. The police could not afford for anyone else to find the body. Especially if there were another decapitation involved. The press would surely have a field day with that.

The first murder had already attracted regional attention. There was no doubt in Robbins mind that a second murder would gain national prominence. If his body was found, in fact, with it's head severed, there would be talk of a serial killer. That was the last thing this particular detective wanted to think about. Serial killer meant one thing. The FBI. The FBI would be called in. They would send some hot shot profiler to Knoxville to assist in the investigation. That usually left the locals 'riding shotgun' the rest of the way. The FBI had no trouble whatsoever when it came to stomping all over any local department's jurisdiction.

The prospect of that scenario made Robbins sick to his stomach. He knew perfectly well who would be sent. The same bastard that let James off the hook some years back. He hated Agent Sandy Borden nearly as much as he hated James. He wasn't sure if he could even work jointly with Borden again. They were on opposite sides of the spectrum. Borden being one of those touchy-feely, psychologically motivated sensitive types. Whereas Robbins had no feelings for anyone or anything. Everything was essentially black and white to him.

His adversaries had used that theory of 'black and white' to express why Robbins was limited as an investigator. They believe he lacked the creativity and lateral thinking to be truly successful. Anyone, they argued, could follow concrete clues and evidence. The real masters, like Agent Sandy Borden, could improvise and speculate.

Robbins was happy being a dinosaur and had absolutely no intentions of changing to fit in with the modern world. He would rather be let go than compromise his Neanderthal work ethic. The latter may very well be the case if he didn't come up with something substantial on this one and soon. The clock was ticking.

Chapter 37

After spending the better part of the morning calling and visiting the people on his list, Frank finally headed toward the deli. The show must go on despite the recent events. Besides, he couldn't think of anything else he could do to safeguard himself, his friends and his family. He couldn't let this take over his life completely. He had come to far to be sidetracked now.

Marco arrived fifteen minutes after James and the two men began their assault on the day's 'to-do' list. They would be receiving two large truckloads of goods. One from Sysco and the other from Institutional Jobbers. I.J. was the only food distributor that could deliver the quality and types of meats that James wanted. He would settle for nothing less than Boar's Head luncheon meats.

James was more than satisfied with the progress of the physical appearance of the restaurant. It was almost completely intact. What he really needed was prospective employees. As of today, his staff consisted of Marco and himself as the full timers, with Carl Metcalf and his sister Rose doing some part time work. That wouldn't do. He needed at least one more full time employee. He needed people that were going to be there more often than not. That is how long-standing relationships with the guests are developed. Too many part time employees takes away from the consistency of a business.

Training was an issue as well. The Knuckle Sandwich Deli was slated to open on the seventeenth of June. That was no random date. It would be the three year anniversary of Frank putting down alcohol and drugs. A smooth opening would be an incredible gift. Tangible evidence that his new way of life was paying off dividends.

With three weeks to go, there was not much time left for training his staff. If people didn't start to show up, he would have to get a bit more proactive in the hiring process. He was no stranger to looking for help. When he was working in the bigger cities with Hooters, he would frequent other restaurants trying to recruit for his place. That was on the borderline of 'ethical' and 'not so much'.

Frank was putting the last of the Boar's Head cold cuts in the deli coolers when the front door swung open. He looked up in disbelief. His heart racing. Palms instantly clammy. He pinched himself to make sure he wasn't dreaming.

"What can I do for you?"

"I heard there was a new restaurant opening here soon. I thought I'd check it out for myself."

"Well, you heard right. If you have any questions, I'm the man to ask.

"Know-it-all, huh?"

Frank smiled. He could never get a break. He was wrapped around her little finger. Frank couldn't think of a comeback. That was unusual. He usually could match sarcastic remarks with the best of them.

Tina moved closer to Frank. "Surprised to see me?"

"You have no idea," he said. Tears welling up in his eyes. It had been just over three years since he'd laid eyes on this woman.

"I got your message and you sounded kind of frantic. What's going on?"

"Weird things are happening. Bad things."

"Well, are you gonna make me guess?"

"I'm sorry, baby. Please sit down. I'll get us a drink. I'll fill you in on everything I know."

Chapter 38

Tina sat quietly. Staring at Frank with a blank expression, she tried to comprehend all that he had just unloaded on her. Drama. It surrounded him constantly. Maybe it wouldn't matter if he was sober or not.

"Say something Tina."

"Like what?"

"Like anything. What are you thinking right now?"

"I'm thinking that you're a freakin' disaster magnet."

"I didn't have…"

"I know! I know! You didn't have anything to do with this. Right? How many times have I heard that before?"

"Look! I'm not the same person I was. Exactly what part I play in this is unclear at this time. My only reason for telling you all this is because I don't want anything to happen to you. I couldn't take it. I just want you to be very careful. Don't talk to strangers. Watch out for anything out of the ordinary. Try not to be alone at night. In or out of the house."

"Great! You screwed someone over, they've returned to get even and I'm the one who has to change my life! Where's the fucking justice in that? Can you tell me that?"

"There is none, baby. I'm doing everything I can to get to the bottom of this."

"Frank… where's the invoice for the dry goods? Oh! Sorry. I didn't know you were busy."

"No, that's fine. Marco, this is my… friend… Tina. Tina…

Marco. He's gonna be my right hand man."

"Oh yeah, the one in the pictures. Frank's told me a little about you."

"Don't believe too much he says Marco. He's got a Master's degree in bullshit." Tina smirked as she looked at Frank out of the corner of her eye.

"Can't prove that by me. He's been like a Godsend to me. Gave me a job. A place to live. Seems like he's been pretty straight with me. As a matter of fact, he's gone above and beyond what the average boss would do."

"Hmm… you've got him trained well, don't you Frank?"

"The invoice is in the office by the fax machine. I'll be back in a minute to help you."

"Take your time. Nice to meet you Tina. Look forward to seeing you again real soon." With that, Marco headed to the back. This had been a good day. He was certain he had just found another target. Not just any target. The one that would bring James to his knees.

Tina could see that she was taking her toll on Frank. She knew he was trying hard. That he was sincerely looking out for her. God, how she loved him. She couldn't understand how it was so easy for her to beat him up with words of hate. It wasn't her intention.

"I'm sorry, Frank. I didn't mean to say those things. I know you're just looking out for me. I guess I still have a little anger and resentment from the past."

"Yeah, it's okay. You're not giving me anything I don't deserve."

"Stop it Frank! You don't deserve it. That's the point. You sure as hell used to, but no more." She put her hand up to his face. The heat from her hand felt so good. "Baby," she said.

That took all the breath out of Frank's body. How he wanted to hold her. That might be too forward right now. He would settle for her hand. He'd waited three long years for her to call him baby once again.

Tina stepped back. "The place looks great, Frank. Really, I'm impressed."

"Yeah. It's really coming along. Supposed to open up in about three weeks. You still gonna be my first customer?"

"You bet! Look, I've got to run." She took his face in her hands and delivered a soft, lingering kiss to his lips. "You be careful, too. I already lost you once. I don't know if I could handle it again."

"I will. You, too. I'll call you later to see if you're okay."

"Alright. Bye Frank."

Frank stood there seemingly paralyzed by Tina's show of affection. A flood of emotions overcame him. Love. Hope. Confidence. Fear. And pity. Pity for anyone that tried to harm one hair on her head. He had learned to remove aggression and revenge from his daily life, thanks to the fellowship of AA. At that moment, however, he realized if anything happened to her... all bets were off.

Chapter 39

Detective Austin Coulter had been Benny Robbins' gopher since he was promoted to the rank of detective. That wasn't the intention when he was teamed with Robbins. He was supposed to be somewhat of a mentor to Coulter. Robbins was not built that way. He lacked the communication skills to teach. That was for sure. But his real inability to teach stemmed from the irrefutable fact that he could care less about anyone but himself. His argument was that if someone was unable to figure things out on their own, they simply were not suited for the job.

Coulter resented this miserable bastard more than words could express. That was why it gave him great pleasure to be the messenger of some potentially upsetting news for Robbins. The Sheriff himself wanted to see Robbins... and he was not happy.

Robbins returned to the squad room in a foul mood himself. He had just returned from the scene where Johnny Tattoo's body was found. The killer thought it would be fun to pose the body on a bench in the courtyard at the center of the Federal Building. It just sat there with it's legs crossed and it's head sitting in his hands across his lap. The bastard was mocking the entire Sheriff's Department.

Benny Robbins looked at it as an invitation for a certain federal agency to join in the hunt. That would be his worst fear come true. It would bring him face to face with his nemesis, Sandy Borden.

Relishing Robbins' present state of frustration and dispair, Austin Coulter pranced up to him sitting at his desk. "Benny, the Sheriff was here looking for you. He seemed pretty ornery."

"Well that's just the icing on the cake of my fuckin' day!"

"He wanted you in his office as soon as you… and I quote…'get yer big, fat twinkie-eatin' ass back here. I think that means now."

Robbins cringed. Coulter celebrated with large amounts of 'inner laughter.' Knowing just the right buttons to push, Coulter continued his assault. "That sure was something, dumpin' the body right there in the middle of Federal Plaza. He's got some balls."

"What? Are you a fucking fan now?"

"Naw! I's jest sayin' he's got some balls is all." Coulter blurted in his best country subservient accent. Knowing full well that Robbins would catch the sarcasm.

"Well keep your damn comments to yourself. I don't need some snot-nosed little puke like you rubbing my nose in it."

"Didn't mean nuttin' by it, Benny. I's sure yer doin' yer best. 'Member, I'm on yer side! Hell, it's like I'm Luke Skywalker and yer my Yoda!" Coulter walked away before he was consumed by side-splitting laughter.

"That's just great. Fuckin' Yoda! Poor inbred bastard."

Chapter 40

Robbins timidly approached his cousin's office and half-heartedly knocked on the door.

"Come in."

"You wanted to see me, cousin?"

"Don't you give me that cousin bullshit! Nothing, not even me, is going to save your sorry ass if you mess this one up."

Looking down at his shoes, Robbins managed to mumble a weak, "Yes, sir."

"This ain't no time to get pitiful, Benny. I need you to be sharp. And fast. The damn Mayor is all over my ass on this one. This friggin' place will be crawlin with Feds by the end of the week if we don't produce some leads. So... tell me you have something."

"Besides both victims being decapitated, we have found one other common piece of evidence. Both victims cell phones were found at the scenes. We checked the phones and discovered that they both made a call right before they were whacked."

"Tell me it gets better than that. Tell me there's some other connection than they both made a damn phone call."

Robbins paused. He was not entirely sure how his cousin would take what he was about to tell him. He was, however, fairly certain he would be less than thrilled by this tidbit of information.

"As a matter of fact, boss, there is more. Both victims called the same person. The first call was captured on the person's voicemail. We even have a copy of the tape."

"How did you get a copy so fast?"

"He delivered it to us the day that Samantha Sullivan's body was found. The actual murder was caught on tape. Chainsaw and everything."

"And the second call?"

"The second call was actually answered by this man. He called and talked to Sergeant Huggins early this morning. Supposedly he was on the line to hear this murder in progress. I haven't spoken to him myself as of yet."

"Why the hell not?"

"Well, the body showed up in the courtyard at Federal Plaza and I've been just a bit preoccupied up until now. I just learned of the call when I returned here a few minutes ago. Since then, you and I have been bonding."

"Don't try and be a smart ass with me you smug little son-of-a-bitch. I made you! I've saved you from the chopping block! Don't, for one minute, think that I can't destroy you just as easily. Do you understand me?"

"Yes, Sir." What Benny wouldn't have given for a lagre, serrated hunting knife at this very moment. He was sick to death of this weasel reminding him that he was his creation.

"Alright then! End the suspense. Who is this man that has been privy to both murders? Or shouldn't I ask? The name is going to give me an ulser, isn't it?"

"You won't be alone. I can assure you of that."

Robbins took a deep breath and prepared himself for the rage about to be rained down on him. He would rather have been anywhere else in the world right at this moment other than here.

"Frank James."

Chapter 41

Sheriff Sanders leaned forward and rested his forehead on the large, mahogany desk he was perched behind. The awkward moment of silence was broken when he began to slowly, but firmly, bang his head against the desktop.

Not knowing how to respond to this outburst by his powerful, albeit deranged cousin, Robbins decided to let him vent his frustration in this rather unorthodox manner. Half of him hoping that this would subdue his anger. The other half hoping this would knock him out cold. Either option relieving the brunt of the animosity that would surely be aimed at him.

Slowly returning upright, Sanders softly spoke. "Tell me you're kidding. Please. Tell me this is your idea of a bad joke. A really bad, sick joke."

"I wish I could, cousin. But I can't. It's a fact. It floored me as well when I first discovered it."

"You had better be straight with me on this one, Benny. If you think for one second that putting James in the middle of this will in some way give you a sense of redemption for what happened between you two in the past, you've got another thing coming."

"Look! He came to me. Not the other way around. I'm not saying he's guilty. Hell, I'm not even saying he's a suspect at this juncture. The only thing I know is that he's the only connection we have right now."

Robbins paused and looked his cousin straight in the eyes. "We both know I hate that mother fucker. Nothing would please me more than to put his ass away for life. But... I hate people getting their heads chopped off more. I want it to stop. I want to be the one to stop it. If James is involved, I'll find out. Believe me! My dick gets hard hoping he's the one doing this shit. But, there is no redemption if he's innocent and other people die due to my own negligence and obsession with some personal vendetta against that asshole."

Sanders studied his underling. He decided to give Robbins just enough rope to hang himself. He had learned to put nothing past his cousin. He would destroy anyone or anything to save his ass. "Very well, Detective. Keep me updated constantly. I don't want to have to read about this investigation in the News-Sentinel. That will be all."

Robbins was impressed with his performance. For a minute there, he almost had himself believing that he lived for truth, justice and the American way. Anyone who had ever come in contact with him would know different. He was all about himself. Himself... and destroying Frank James once and for all.

Chapter 42

Allison O'Callahan led a pretty simple life. Although she would have liked people to believe her world revolved around her twelve year old son, Matty, that was not the case. It hadn't been the case for some time. The painful truth was that her world revolved around her need for alcohol. Everyone and everything else in her life were positioned below alcohol on her priority list. If she were to try, she probably would be unable to pinpoint the exact date where she became prisoner to alcohol. That's probably the reason she never tried.

She had been drinking alcoholically for years. Alcohol became more and more necessary to function on a day to day basis. Fortunately for her, drinking was an acceptable part of her chosen profession. She was a bartender. The alcoholic's dream job. Encouraged by management to indulge in cocktails with customers because that added money to the till. Allison did it for selfish reasons. The high, at first, obsessed her thoughts. Next came the compulsion to drink. At this stage of the game, however, it was purely maintenance drinking. Any attempt to stop or even reduce her use would lead to a severe case of delirium tremens. The *DT's* as they are more commonly referred to. Any alcoholic that has ever been exposed to these would rather have their life snuffed out than to have these tremors last for any significant amount of time.

The thing that let Allison continue this insane assault on her liver was the fact that she was one of the few alcoholics that didn't get mean on booze. The more she sat on the barstool, the more placid she became. She was everybody's pal. There was no one she couldn't hold a conversation with. All who crossed her path perceived her to be a sweet girl that just liked to drink a little. And that she was. Until she got home. If she didn't pass right out after work, then she could be counted on to offer up some verbal abuse to anyone who was within earshot. Anyone who was close to her. Anyone who was there to help. Those were the people that she attacked.

Anyone who took a chance on getting close to her would leave skid marks before long. They couldn't run fast enough. This allowed Allison to involve herself in relationships on a purely superficial level. Many acquaintences, but almost no true friends. That was the way she liked it. Not much of a chance for her nasty little secret to get brought out into the open. She was content to live her life on a steady diet of loneliness and one night stands. No desire to understand, and even less to be understood.

She was perhaps the most pitiful type of all of the alcoholics. Constantly using the drink to cover up any pain, emotion or fear that she chose not to address. Having her share of ups and downs, but nothing that brought about consequences harsh enough for her to take a look at her addiction. These types were generally in for years and years of useless and unnecessary suffering. Feeling in control of her life, yet unable and unwilling to realize the extent of her vulnerability. A vulnerability that, in all likelyhood, would land her in one of three places… jails, institutions or death.

Chapter 43

"Marco, come in here a minute."

Marco wandered into the main dining room and saw Frank James standing next to a tall, gangly dark haired boy. "What's up, Frank?"

"This is Scott Willow. He likes to go by Scrappy. He's going to be joining us full time. I also hired that girl, Sara Evans. She was the cute little brunette that was here earlier. I think her perky personality will be perfect for the register. Me, you and Scrappy here can take care of the rest. What do you think?"

"That's great. But, why Scrappy?"

The seemingly prepubescent, pimply-faced youngster's chest swelled up as he peered directly into Marco's eyes. "Because I don't take anybody's shit. People look at me and think they can intimidate me or take advantage of me because of my size. I don't take kindly to that and have no problem letting them know about it. My parents would be called into school two or three times a week because I popped someone in the beak. So, they started calling me Scrappy because I fought so much."

James smiled. He like this kid. A little attitude never hurt anyone. Scrappy reminded him a little of himself when he was very young. He was pleased with the two additions he made to his staff today.

The three of them stood and talked, trying to get to know each other a bit. Frank explained what he wanted out of his people. He also asked them their expectations of him. As they were speaking, Frank noticed that a black Crown Victoria, followed by two Knox

County Sheriff cruisers, had pulled up in front of the deli. He told Marco to take Scrappy and give him a detailed tour of the place. He didn't want to scare off the kid before he started. This confrontation might very well have done just that.

Frank closed his eyes,took a deep breath, and tried to prepare himself as best he could to deal with the sorry excuse for a detective that was coming in his front door.

Chapter 44

Troncillo racked the balls for yet another game of eight ball while Javier went to the bar to grab two more Heinekens from the cute red-headed bartender that had been so nice to them all afternoon. They had played themselves off as golfers on their way to Charleston to indulge in the low country's premier courses. They dressed the part from their pastel polos, right down to their matching Ping golf caps.

They noticed right away that this girl kept eyeballing them from behind the bar ever since they had arrived at The Corner Pocket. Earlier in the day they had taken a break from the pool table and bellied up to the bar for some chicken wings. She was sweet and attentive to both of them, but seemed to have a little something extra for Javier. That would be what they used to get their foot in the door with her.

They began wetting her appetite, as well as her whistle, with several rounds of shots and some harmless flirting. The two men didn't have a lot of time to work with. They needed to be somewhat aggressive, but not so much as to scare her off. Escobar had given them specific orders to take care of their latest target without haste. He wanted them in and out of South Carolina, having minimal contact with the people of Greenville. Minimum contact meant a lesser chance of them being remembered or implicated in the deed they were about to pull off.

Allison felt those familiar lustful desires that usually came to her after she was half lit. The fact that these handsome strangers were just passing through made them even more desirable. She could satisfy her sexual appetite without any strings attached. She had been putting on her best 'Southern Belle' act all day and was reasonably sure that they were interested.

She wondered if it would be possible to get the one called Javier to abandon his friend for the night. *What the hell*, she thought. If it came right down to it, she would invite them both back to her place. It wouldn't be the first time she'd been with more than one man at the same time. Besides, Matty was with his father in Columbia. They would not be back until sometime tomorrow evening.

Allison placed the Heinekens on the bar in front of Javier. She batted her eyes and asked if he had plans for the night. He told her he had nothing special going on, but felt kind of weird leaving his friend all alone in a strange town. Otherwise, he would absolutely love to spend some time together. Having already anticipated that response, as well as it's solution, Allison said the invitation was good for the both of them. Southern hospitality and all. A wide grin stretched across Javier's face. Allison matched him grin for grin. Both equally excited about the wild ride ahead of them. Unfortunately for Allison, she had no idea it would be her last ride. Just then, Javier felt a pang of sadness. He liked this girl. She had done nothing to deserve what was coming her way on this fateful night.

He forced those thoughts out of his mind and quickly got back into character. Orders were made to be obeyed. Javier also knew what would happen to both he and Troncillo if their mission was not carried out.

With a sly wink to Allison, Javier headed back to the pool table to let Troncillo in on the good news. It was time to hammer out the details of their upcoming excursion.

Allison felt a rush of moisture between her thighs in anticipation of what she figured would be an insatiable night of lust and alcohol. After tonight, she was sure she could go months before she would need another sexual fix. She had no way of knowing this would be the end of the road. Tonight she would leave behind two grieving parents and a son whose innocence would be lost forever.

Chapter 45

As Robbins waddled through the door, Frank noticed his newly sprouted goatee and had to supress his laughter. He was reminded of Avery Schreiber. Schreiber was the rumpled slob of a man that used to appear in the old Doritos commercials..

Robbins took his position right in front of James, while the four uniformed Deputies he brought as back up fanned out to surround James completely. Frank did not like the way this was playing out already. Surely this much firepower would not be necessary for an ordinary questioning session.

"I've been expecting you, Benny. What took you so long?"

"Been a little busy cleaning up dead bodies."

"Any leads?"

"Funny you should ask, asshole. You seem to know more than us. Why is that exactly? Do we have any leads? Yeah…and they all lead us back to you."

"What the hell are you talking about? Just because they both called me? Get serious. I don't know why they called, but I can guarantee I didn't have anything to do with their murders."

"Do you have an alibi?"

"I was home in bed when Johnny called. He woke me up. I called you shortly after that. Why the hell do you think I would offer this information if I was somehow involved in this mess?"

"That's what I'm trying to figure out. What about Sullivan? You didn't answer that time. Maybe she called your number to lead us to her killer. That wouldn't be the first time, Frankie-boy. What happened? She wasn't hungry for the Italian sausage, so you had to get a little rough?"

James could feel his blood pressure rising. He had to keep himself in check. Robbins was trying to throw him off his game. He was baiting him. That was what the Deputies were there for. He was hoping to get James to act up so they could arrest him on the spot.

Robbins stood with his arms crossed, resting them on his flabby midsection. "There wouldn't happen to be anyone who could corroborate your whereabouts on either occasion by any chance?"

"I was working alone the night Samantha was killed. I'd left my phone at the house or I would have answered that call too."

Robbins smiled, "That sucks for you!" He wanted to see James squirm. "What about the night your scumbag friend Johnny bit the big one?"

"You're a real bastard, Benny. You couldn't have even been a pimple on Johnny's ass and you know it!"

"Quit your damn whining and answer the question."

At that moment, James realized that he had forgotten all about his new roommate. "As a matter of fact, I do have someone. I recently hired a new guy to be my right hand man around here. He didn't have a place to stay, so I'm letting him have my spare bedroom. We were both home all night."

Robbins frowned over this tidbit of information, but continued without hesitation. He would not let James have the satisfaction of seeing even the slightest bit of disappointment on his face. "I guess I'll have to have a word with your new flunky. Let's hope it's not a case of you lie and Bozo swears to it."

"I've got no reason to lie."

"Sure you don't. You're such an upstanding citizen and all. Let me tell you something, asswipe. Just because you're not smoking crack and you somehow managed to open your stupid little deli here, it doesn't mean you've changed. You were a no good, dirty rotten scumbag when I first laid eyes on you, and, from where I'm standing, you still are."

"That means a lot coming from such a fat, lazy, sorry excuse for a human being like you, Benny. And let me tell you something. I've worked my ass off to change. It took courage and honesty unlike anything I've ever done in my life. So I've earned everything I have today. I know that's hard for you to comprehend. How hard did you have to work to get where you are, by the way?"

Benny's jowls turned a dark shade of red. His temples started to throb. He knew where James was going with this. It would be a slap in the face to Robbins if James said what he thought he was about to say. Especially in front of the Deputies that had accompanied the him here today. The Detective was about to redirect the conversation, but was too late. Frank hit him with both barrels.

"Oh… that's right… your cousin got you the job. If it wasn't for him, you'd still be getting cups of piss thrown on you by the inmates at the Penal Farm. How nice it must be to have family."

Frank scanned the room with his eyes. Immediately he saw that his last comment had gotten the desired response he was shooting for. Each of the four Deputies stood with mangled faces trying to hold back the laughter. Frank knew these Deputies despised Robbins for what he was and how he came to power. Now, Robbins had to feel the anger and resentment first hand.

Continuing his assault on Robbins, Frank said, "Now… if you're not taking me in and you have no more questions… get the hell outta here! I've got work to do."

Completely embarrassed and frustrated, Detective Robbins retreated towards the exit. As he reached the door, he turned to James. "Don't plan on any vacations in the immediate future. I don't believe you or trust you, and I'm going to do whatever it takes to get your ass this time. Got me?"

"You know, Benny… you were much more intimidating without the chin pubes."

James stood smiling. He knew damn well that Robbins would be cursing him all the way down I-40. Sometimes it is the little things that help you to get through the day.

Chapter 46

Agent Sandy Borden was a company man. He loved his job. Hell, he was the job. That became evident when his wife, Jenny, left him and took their son, Eddie, with her. She had told him for years that she loved him, but felt he never had time for her and Eddie. She cried when she left because she still loved him so, but he had given his heart to someone else.

How Jenny wished it had been another woman. She would have been able to compete with another human being. Against the job she stood no chance. She'd hoped her leaving would snap Sandy out of it. Make him realize what was important in life. That was the plan, but boy did it backfire. Borden sank himself deeper and deeper into his work. Oblivious to the pain he caused himself and his family.

At six feet four inches tall and one hundred eighty-five pounds, Borden was by no means physically imposing. It was his confidant swagger and uncanny ability to see through the bullshit that seemed to intimidate people. Those traits were largely responsible for his meteoric rise to the top of his field. He was moved to the FBI's Special Homicides Division after spending a mere two years as a regular field agent.

While his promotion was unprecedented throughout the history of the FBI, it was his success on a grisly murder case in North Carolina six months later that would etch his name in FBI folklore forever. He would be known as the man who single-handedly took down the serial killer they called the Angel of Death.

The Angel of Death was a North Carolina businessman named Carson Condon. He was a pathetic man whose wife left him because he was unable to have children. After that, he blamed innocent children for the miserable existence he called life.

Condon began carrying out orders that he would later claim were given to him by an 'Angel that descended from the Heavens.' He abducted and tortured thirteen young girls between the ages of six and nine. When their poor, fragile bodies could take no more punishment or abuse, he smothered them, dressed them up all in white, stapled an aluminum foil halo to the back of their heads and left them to be discovered by the authorities.

Agent Borden took it upon himself to not sleep until this monster was caught. He studied every crime scene, every victim's bedroom, their common traits anything and everything that could help put an end to the horrific crime spree.

In a matter of five weeks, Borden managed to make the connection between the missing girls and the candy store owned by Condon. He posted up in a bookstore directly across the street and kept an eye on him. One day, a little girl wandered in to the store by herself. A few minutes after the girl entered the store, Condon locked the door and flipped the open sign to closed.

When Borden approached the door, he heard a muffled scream. That was all the probable cause he needed. He grabbed a trash can off the street and sent it crashing through the pane of glass that served as a front door. Spotting the little girls hat on the floor near the magazine rack, Borden began searching for stairs or an office. Any place this sick monster could possibly have taken the poor child. He could find nothing. No office. No rear entrance. Nothing.

Frustration and rage began to take over. He was so close, yet so far. That's when he got a lucky break. A loud , crashing noise that sounded like someone falling down stairs. But how? There were no stairs. None that he could find. Borden hung his head in desperation. From the corner of his eye, he thought he saw a mouse disappear behind the heavy wooden magazine rack. One push on the side of the rack was all it took. The entire unit slid effortlessly, revealing a secret passageway that led to a dark staircase. Borden slowly descended the steps with his revolver drawn.

When he reached the bottom, he came face to face with the animal who had been wreaking havoc on this quiet town nestled in the foothills of the Smokey Mountains. He raised his weapon, identifying himself as FBI and commanded Condon to back away from the girl. Knowing it was the end of his run, Condon lurched for the hunting knife resting on the table next to him. One hand on the knife and the other trying to bring the girl in front of him for a shield. Before he could get the girl to get off the floor, Borden placed a slug into his shoulder, sending him toppling back over a pile of pillows and blankets.

Everything in Borden wanted to finish off the miserable excuse for a human being that lay still in a puddle of his own blood. He placed the barrel of his revolver to Condon's forehead. At that moment, he saw that Condon's eyes were pleading for him to end his suffering. There was no way he was going to let him get off the hook that easy. Borden wanted Condon to experience pain and suffering equal to that of his victims. Although he knew in his heart that it may never be entirely possible.

With Condon put away, Borden became the new golden boy of the FBI. He could choose his destiny. It was just a few weeks later that he became a serial profiler. He had arrived.

Chapter 47

A gent Borden couldn't believe it had been eighteen years since he began his journey. He had seen more murder and mayhem than any one man should be privy to in a lifetime. Times ten. Most people would have gotten out long ago. Not him. He seemed to have been born for this.

He had wondered how long it would take the higher-ups to assign him to the murders going on in Knoxville. Borden had been keeping an eye on it ever since the first body was found. He figured they were waiting as long as possible because of the relationship between Borden and Benny Robbins, the lead detective in charge of the investigation for the Knox County Sheriff's Department. Lack of relationship would be more accurate. Robbins hated him ever since he stepped on Robbins' toes in the investigation of a major Southeastern cocaine ring that was based in Knoxville. Robbins was unable to function effectively because of his hell bent desire to pin everything on a man named Frank James.

Agent Borden came in and took over the case. He used Frank James to catch the real masterminds behind the drug ring. The real slap in the face to Robbins occurred when, on Borden's recommendation, a Federal Judge granted James immunity for his involvement with the drug cartel because of his cooperation and assistance in bringing them all down. Robbins hated both men and vowed to exact revenge if it was the last thing he did.

Well, all that didn't matter anymore. The minute they found a body in Greenville, South Carolina that had been decapitated and posed out in public with the victim's head in her hands, the FBI took over. Anytime an investigation crossed state lines, the Feds were called in. Borden had gotten the call at breakfast. A chopper had landed in Columbia, South Carolina thirty minutes later to whisk him off to Greenville. The flight took all of twenty six minutes. A rental awaited him on the tarmack of Donaldson Airport in Greenville. Within minutes, he was on his way to Furman University. The body had been discovered seated in a chair in the ampitheater by the lake on Furman's campus. It was found about seven thirty in the morning by a pair of freshman joggers.

Several State Police cruisers lined the narrow road that accessed the amphitheater. There were also dozens of uniformed officers and campus security guards fanned out to keep the ever growing crowd of spectators at bay. Borden liked to call them 'ghoul hounds.' He was amazed at how many people would flock from all around with the hopes of seeing a little gore. Preying on and feeding off someone else's misery and misfortune. Borden was reasonably sure that if any one of these ghoul hounds were to get within two feet of the victim, they would be cured of their morbid fascinations forever.

Agent Borden showed the trooper in charge his credentials and passed under the yellow police tape that created a perimeter around the crime scene. Bile rose in his throat as he approached the blood spattered stage and looked into the lifeless eyes of the latest victim of the Headless Horseman. That was the label the media had already given the killer after the second body was found in Knoxville. Borden could already see tomorrow's headline: "THE HEADLESS HORSEMAN RIDES AGAIN!"

Chapter 48

You could have heard a pin drop in the Detective Division's squad room at the Knox Count Sheriff's Department on this final day in May. Every seat behind every desk filled. The entire division anxiously anticipating the show that was sure to begin in a matter of seconds. They watched enthusiastically as Detective Benny Robbins closed the door behind him as he entered Captain Shubert's office.

There was no love loss between the Captain and his underling. Actually, Shubert seemed to make it his own personal crusade to belittle Robbins every chance he got. He made absolutely no bones about the fact that he considered Robbins' entire tenure as Detective a complete and utter travesty of justice. He often told Robbins that if it weren't for his cousin, he would surely be pumping gas or washing dishes for a living.

There was no doubt that Shubert was thrilled to be the one to deliver what he hoped was a knockout blow to Benny Robbins. He felt like a child at Christmas given the gift of being the messenger of doom to this gigantic pain in the ass. Exposing Robbins' Achilles heel. Even his cousin, the legendary Sheriff Sanders, could not save him on this one. Shubert absolutely believed that even winning the Mega Millions Lottery would place a distant second on the list of things that would make him truly happy.

"You wanted to see me, Captain?" Robbins did his best to remain professional and somewhat cordial. Everything inside him wanted to tell the Captain exactly what he thought of having to see him first thing in the morning. Hell, his breakfast hadn't even begun digesting yet. This was part of the job, however. Robbins decided his juicy expletives would be best saved for a later date.

Captain Shubert gave Robbins a gleaming smile. "Please, have a seat Benny," Shubert said while motioning to a folding chair directly in front of his mammoth mahogany desk. He had that chair brought in especially for this occasion. It looked like something that belonged behind an elementary school desk. Robbins actually had to look up at his Captain, further solidifying his role as the submissive.

"Have you been watching the news? It seems there has been another development in your latest case. Police in Greenville, South Carolina found a body on the campus of Furman University. A young lady named Allison O'Callahan. Apparently she's the latest victim of your boy."

Robbins appeared to be unphased at this juncture of the conversation. "And just what makes those Greenville yahoos think this is my guy?"

"Well, for starters, she was holding her head in her hands. Even you would have to see that there may be some correlation."

"Purely circumstantial! Any old Tom, Dick or Harry could have done that and made it look like my guy. They figure that let's them off the hook. Maybe you shouldn't believe everything you hear on television. It wouldn't be the first time one of those news lady bimbos have exaggerated and totally misinterpreted information. Gimme a friggin' break!"

"She got the information from the South Carolina State Troopers. How in the hell could she misinterpret the facts. Are you saying the Troopers don't know what they are doing?"

Robbins puffed out his chest. "I'm just sayin' let the real detectives do the work. It takes very little vision on the part of the Carolina State Troopers to chalk it up to my guy. That means it's not their problem. It's mine. They're freed up to give some more damn speeding tickets. Maybe catch a couple of real criminals not wearing their seatbelts. Just because the girl's head was chopped off, that doesn't automatically connect the murders. Maybe they should have some professionals do a complete sweep of the crime scene."

This was getting good for Shubert. Robbins was digging himself a hole that he would be unable to escape. Shubert really should not have been enjoying this as much as he was. Too bad. He loved it. The Captain took a deep breath and delivered the equivalent of a stiff blow to the solar plexus. "Oh yeah! There was one more thing. They found a picture of the girl standing with a man outside Tommy Condon's Pub in Charleston. It was right there on her lap, next to her head."

"See that! I told you this wasn't related. My guy uses cell phones as clues. A very important oversight by this sick-ass copycat killer." With that, Robbins stood up and put on his very best smug face. "Anything else, Skipper?"

Here it was. The moment of truth. The proverbial knockout punch. Shubert wished he had been videotaping this entire conversation. He would play it any time he was feeling down. "The man in the picture was Frank James."

Dead silence. A popular television commercial came to Shubert's mind immediately. 'The Twinkie Robbins probably had in his pocket...sixty cents. The dry cleaning bill to get the grease spots out of the Detective's buttondown oxford... twelve bucks. The look on Detective Benny Robbins' face right at this very moment... PRICELESS!'

Chapter 49

Never, in his entire career with the Knox County Sheriff's Department, had Shubert's workday began on such a high note. Absolutely delightful. Seeing this slovenly excuse for a human being on the brink of a meltdown seemed to warm the cockles of his heart. Professionalism should have dictated that he show his subordinate some compassion and understanding at this juncture of the discussion. It should have, but sarcasm and spitefullness won out. They usually did. Especially when dealing with the likes of Robbins.

"Are you alright, Benny? You look like you are gonna lose your breakfast. Can I get you a cold towel? A waste basket, perhaps?"

Robbins had to regain his composure. He needed to shake off the numbness that seemed to take over his body. He started with his head and let the ripple work it's way down his entire frame. His body shuddered like that of a dog that had just been given a bath. Robbins took a deep breath and glared at Shubert. "You're enjoying the hell out of this, aren't you?"

"Well, Benny, they say every cloud has it's silver lining. You've certainly been my cloud. So, yeah, I'm loving this. I'm anxious to see if you'll deal with this yourself, or look for some divine intervention from a few floors up."

"I can handle myself. I don't need any help from anyone around here."

Shubert smiled. "Funny you should say that, Detective. You are not the only one that believes there is no one around here that can help you. So, as of today, you will be sharing the lead in this investigation with someone outside the Sheriff's Department. It shouldn't be too hard for you. You'll be working closely with an old friend of yours. The FBI has decided to send your old pal Sandy Borden to bail your ass out once again.

"No freaking way! I cannot work with that son-of-a-bitch. You know that and I know that."

"You can and you will! Make no mistake about that. The only way you will get out of this is to resign and leave your badge and gun on my desk before you go out there and clean off your desk. Got me?"

"I got you. I'll get even with you one of these days, Shubert. I'm getting real tired of you pushing me around all the time."

"Cry me a river you fuckin' baby! Take your best shot. I recommend, however, that you focus all your energy on catching whoever it is that is slashing the heads off people that we're supposed to 'protect and serve.' That's a little more important than going off on yet another personal vendetta of revenge."

Robbins bowed his head. How he would love to put a bullet in his Captain's forehead. That thought made him smile. He looked Shubert in the eyes. "Yes, Sir. By the way, when can I expect to be graced by Borden's presence?"

"He's wrapping things up in Greenville and should be here after lunch. His flight comes in at 2:30PM at McGhee-Tyson. I thought it would be a nice gesture for you to meet him at the airport. He'll be expecting you."

Shubert smiled as Robbins' face turned beet red. He was reminded of an old horror flick called 'Scanners.' All that was missing were the large, thick, pulsing veins throughout Robbins' head and face that would eventually erupt, causing his head to explode. What an ideal way to end this whole ordeal.

With his shoulders hunched over, Robbins took his leave from the Captain's office. Shubert was feeling all warm and fuzzy inside. His day had been made. Without hesitation, he picked up the phone and dialed his wife. He thought he would take her out to lunch and make her day. He would 'pay it forward,' so to speak. Not even she would be able to knock him off the pink cloud he was on today.

Chapter 50

Frank James sat in amazement, his eyes glued to the television. With his mouth agape, James sat motionless, trying to process the information CNN was offering it's audience. He couldn't believe his eyes. More accurately, he didn't want to believe his eyes. But, there it was. Right in front of him. Live and in living color. CNN correspondent Summer Breeze describing the footage being shown in her usual somber tone.

Mass amounts of squad cars, patrolmen and spectators were shown encompassing the lakeside amphitheater on the campus of Furman University. There had been a grizzly murder. Early speculation leaned toward this murder being related to those in Knoxville, Tennessee. No name was given for the victim as of yet. They didn't need to. Frank knew in his heart who it was. He became nauseous the instant they showed the signage that announced they were on Furman's campus. Bile rose in his throat when Summer hinted to the connection between this murder and the heinous crimes that had been recently plaguing Knoxville.

While the coverage of the atrocity in South Carolina was still quite generic, James knew it would only be a matter of time before the public would be given the identity of the latest victim of the so-called Headless Horseman. By that time, the powers that be would have already connected him with this victim as well. That's if they hadn't already. There was on more thing that stuck out in his mind as rather odd. He hadn't even thought of it until just now. The phone call. There wasn't one. While he was certainly no authority on serial

115

killers, James was finding it hard to believe the clue that so blatently pointed a finger at him in the first two murders, would be omitted from the third. This oversight allowed him a modicum of hope that there was, in fact, a different killer.

This thought was fleeting, however. The feeling of hope was completely fabricated. James would bet his life that the latest victim was Allison O'Callahan. She was dead simply because she had the misfortune of being part of Frank's past. They weren't even close. The two hadn't spoken since the day James backed out of the driveway of the house they shared on Windsor Drive. The day he ended the tumultuous five years of hell he endured trying to make their relationship work.

The only thing that ever crossed his mind about that time of his life was Allison's son, Matty. That hit James like a ton of bricks. Poor Matty. Frank had been too busy on his own pity-pot to comprehend the fact that that wonderful, innocent boy would be scarred for life by his mother's death.

It infuriated James to think that all this sadness and dismay was due to the fact that some sick son-of-a-bitch made a connection between James and O'Callahan. While the deaths of Johnny Tattoo and Samantha were both horrible and disturbing in their own right, at least the two of them were all alone in life. Many would surely grieve over their deaths. James included. However, it was realistic to believe that life would return to normal shortly after their bodies were put to rest. That was a heartless and incogitable cold, hard fact that would unquestionably have James examining his own humanity.

Allison's death was different. Not only did James have to deal with the guilt of inadvertently being the cause of yet another senseless death, but he was ultimately responsible for the rippling effect of misery and horror that would inexorably become a part of everyday life for Allison's survivors. Her parents would be inconsolable. Matty would be out of his mind with pain and suffering. Frank could actually see her legions of bar regulars forming an unruly mob ready to administer it's own twisted brand of justice to anyone who played a part in Allison's murder. James realized that he, himself, could very well be placed atop that fateful list. He had always been frowned upon as a bad seed by all those bamboozled by Allison's charm. James was never given the luxury of explaining his perspective on any topics or issues that did not completely coincide with her views. To most, he was a nonentity.

That insignificance would soon change. He would be given ample opportunity to try and explain recent events to all sorts of different agencies. The Police, FBI and media immediately came to mind. If, in fact, this murder was directly related to those previously, the FBI was sure to get involved. That would not entirely be a bad thing for James. While it would increase the number of people scrutinizing his every move tenfold, he was almost assured of getting a fairer shake from the Feds than he would by some egotistical incompetent from a backwards Southern law enforcement agency. For all intents and purposes, that egotistical incompetent went by the name of Benny Robbins. The recent developments in South Carolina should have that grumbling, self-serving ass salivating by now.

While his immediate future and personal freedom were uncertain at best, one thing James knew for sure was that he had to have his story down pat. He needed to account for his every move. They would be wanting his alibi, as well as, any witnesses that could substantiaite his claims. He was in for a long, hard ride. Perhaps the most relentless and disturbing ride of his life. That thought was enough to scare the hell out of James, considering some of the ungodly situations he had been in throughout his sordid past.

Chapter 51

The atmosphere at the Knuckle Sandwich Deli was anxious to say the least. Everyone present was unhappily aware of the circumstances that warranted this mandatory staff meeting. There were questions that needed to be answered. Concerns that needed to be addressed. The deli was supposed to be up and running by the seventeenth of June. That meant less than three weeks to get the staff trained on all the equipment and have a full working knowledge of the menu. There needed to be schedules made. Flyers had to be printed and passed out to local hotels and businesses. There was the question of delivery to businesses to help develop the lunch trade. Those were just some of the business oriented issues on the table. The majority of which would be ironed out by themselves, once the more urgent and delicate personal issues involving the owner of the business could be discussed and laid to rest.

That's where Frank planned on starting, so he could get a feel for the crowd. There was no need, or way, to candy coat the things that had occurred recently. Even if there was, it would involve too much tap dancing and expend entirely too much energy. Besides, James had managed to turn his life around by being rigorously honest with himself and others. He would gain absolutely nothing by changing the rules in which he had been accustomed to living. Present the facts, let the chips fall where they may, and decide on a course of action from there.

James took a deep breath as he stood in front of his staff. He was obviously shaken. He knew it and they knew it. Eye contact and confidence would be essential to convey his message and secure their trust. There was nowhere to go but forward. He had worked too hard for his dream to come true. No psycho with a chainsaw was going to take that away from him. The very thought of it gave him a strength that seemed to calm him and temporarily stop his thoughts from reeling.

He spoke. "First off, I would like to thank y'all for coming on such short notice." *Y'all? Christ, I'm becoming a redneck!* "I realize you have other things going on in your lives besides your job here at the deli. I imagine many of you are wondering whether or not your job is secure here. Let me start by making one thing absolutely clear. The Knuckle Sandwich Deli **WILL** open it's doors on June seventeenth. Preferably with all of you being a part of the grand opening. I have chosen you's guys *(there's that Yankeeboy)* because I believe you each have unique qualities that will help to make this place a success. My opinions of you will not waver.

"It is your opinions of me that need to be examined to see if you've made the right choice for employment. I'm gonna cut right to the chase. It's no secret that I am under investigation for potential involvement in the recent murders that have been plaguing our city. I'm here to tell you that I am in no way connected to the sick bastards responsible for those deaths. However, I am involved somewhat. I knew Johnny, Samantha and Allison. She's the latest victim in South Carolina. More than just knew them, actually. I had close personal relationships with all of them."

The room was completely silent. James had their attention. He would give them the facts and let them make their own decisions. Frank took a long swig of his trusty Coca-Cola and continued.

"My name was thrown into the mix because, for some reason, I was the last person both Samantha and Johnny called before they were killed. When I say before, I mean right before. I was actually on the phone when Johnny was killed. I heard the freakin' chainsaw. The call woke me up. I thought I was dreaming. As we all know… I wasn't.

"As for the murder in South Carolina, I am only speculating that the victim's name is Allison. There was no phone call to suggest it is her. However, every bone in my body says it is her. Someone out there wants me to suffer and is killing people that have played an

119

active part in my past. That's my belief. It's not necessarily the police's viewpoint on the subject.

"If you choose to continue here with me, there is a very good chance you will be visited quite frequently by a Detective Benny Robbins. He will question you. He will try to convince you into throwing me under the bus. He may even threaten your freedom and do everything in his power to make all your lives miserable. He will do this because he wants me put away whether I'm guilty or not. He hates me. He thinks I made him look foolish in the face of his peers because the FBI let me off the hook a few years back on drug charges. I cooperated with the Feds and they gave me a second chance. Robbins was furious and will stop at nothing to avenge that slap in the face.

"I'm sure none of you signed up for this kind of drama. You were merely looking for a job. Here's your chance to back out now. No hard feelings. I'll give you two weeks pay to hold you over while you look for another job, give references and anything else that will help you with your transition. If any of you choose to stay, I can only offer you hard work, along with some good old fashioned Police harassment. But… and I mean this with all my heart… you will be in on the ground floor of something I believe is going to be huge. There will be plenty of room for advancement, as well as, financial gain. The goal is to franchise out. Anyone who has what it takes to move this project to the next level will not… and I repeat… NOT be forgotten when we reach the pot of gold at the end of the rainbow. And who knows… we may even develop a little character along the way.

"Take some time to make your decisions. Not too much time, because I need to know where I stand on staffing. If you want to call me, that's fine. I'd prefer to see you all personally. If there is no questions, I guess that will be all."

Scrappy raised his hand and slowly stood. "We don't need time Frank. We already decided if you were straight with us, we would stick it out with you. Besides, it'll be nice to see Robbins eat a nice big shitburger when they find the real killers."

"Is that how the rest of you feel?" Frank anxiously awaited the collective response.

The entire staff stood up and gave James the thumbs up. He was taken aback by this rag-tag group of misfits courage and loyalty. He knew, at that moment, the Knuckle Sandwich Deli was destined for great things.

Chapter 52

It was a typical afternoon at McGhee-Tyson Airport. There was a steady flow of travelers. Some leaving for a tropical paradise, while others were headed for business meetings or seminars in any number of cities that were bound to be more exiting than Knoxville and it's surrounding area. There were, however, an equal amount of business men and women trudging like death row inmates toward several rental car agencies. Each of them less than thrilled to be here. Each of them probably having drawn the short straw at their respective firms.

Then there were the college kids. Young men and women scantily clad in the latest Volunteer summer ware. Staying true to their school even as they headed back to New Jersey, Florida or wherever it was they had left to become part of the intriguing Tennessee Volunteer history that people seemed to obsess over. Half happy to see friends and family without the worry of classes and term papers. Half already longing for the fall semester and the thrill of SEC football.

The only real change at the airport came in the form of beefed-up security. Security that was warranted by post 9/11 paranoia. Still, it felt unnatural. Average civilians not knowing what to be more afraid of, the threat of a terrorist onslaught or the sight of batallions of National Guardsmen pacing the terminals with high-powered automatic weapons. Wondering if their minds were on the job at hand, or if they were preoccupied with thoughts of their families and job security at the local Wal-Mart.

Benny Robbins could have cared less about anyone or anything at the airport on this particular day. It chapped his ass raw that he was here to begin with. He bet Shubert was having a big laugh at his expense right this very minute. The mere thought of coming face to face with Agent Sandy Borden was enough to push his rage meter into the red. That, coupled with the fear of Borden letting James off the hook again, was making him borderline homicidal. He was by no means convinced that James had played a part in the recent Knoxville slayings. Truthfully, that didn't even matter to him. This could very well be the last opportunity Robbins would have to make James suffer for the humiliation he caused him. Detective Benny Robbins wasn't exactly sure what he was capable of to keep James from slipping through his fingers, but there wasn't one single thing he couldn't imagine himself doing at this very moment. No act seemed too despicable. No person not expendable.

Realizing both the time, as well as the fact that he was white knuckling the brass rail that edged the bar at the airport lounge, Robbins slammed back his Wild Turkey 101 and headed off to the gate where his nemesis was due to arrive at any minute. He had no idea how this meeting was going to play out. Should he act like there was no history between him and Borden? Should he be aggressive or passive? He needed to decide what tack would keep Borden off the scent of his revenge. Borden, the ally, would be much more beneficial to him than Borden the enemy. That would take some serious acting on his part. Acting that he was not very confident he could deliver. The very thought of being cordial to that self-righteous bastard caused the Wild Turkey to make it's way back into Robbins' throat. Borden hadn't even landed yet, and was already making Robbins sick to his stomach.

"Flight 2377 from Greenville now arriving at Gate 22," came blaring over the airport intercom. This was it. Showtime. Robbins put on his best fake smile and prepared himself to deliver some good, old-fashioned Southern hospitality to a man for whom he would not shed a single tear for if he was gunned down coming through the terminal doors. Without hesitation, he stammered through the small crowd of people waiting to welcome home their friends and family, making a bee-line to the rather gawky looking Federal Agent that had just arrived.

Chapter 53

"Sandy Borden! How long has it been? Seems like a lifetime since I've seen you. How the hell are you?"

Robbins nearly yanked Borden's arm out of the socket when he wrapped that big meat-hook of a hand around his long, boney fingers, pumping his arm like he was jacking up a Chevy to change a flat tire. Robbins was pleased with the rather alarming look that came over Borden's face. Confusion. Uncertainty. Perhaps even a little fear.

"Hello, Benny. I'm good. I'm good. How about yourself?"

"Couldn't be better. Well, maybe I could if I could catch the sick bastard who's been choppin' off people's heads around here. What I meant to say was I'm really glad you're here. I could damn well use all the help I can get. Ya know? Nip this thing in the bud before any more damage is done."

"That would be nice. That's why I'm here. I guess I'm in a bit of shock over your reception. I totally expected you to feel like... well, mad as hell that we were taking over the lead on this one. I guess I was expecting a left hook as opposed to a hearty handshake."

"Hell, I'd be lying if I said I wasn't a bit angry when I found out you guys were taking over. Who wouldn't be? You know as well as I do that these things get personal. But after you cool down a bit, you start thinking more clearly and realize that the chances of catching this creep increase exponentially when y'all get involved. There are a lot more resources available to the Federal Government than there are to some podunk county agency. When it's all said and done, I

124

have to remind myself that it's not me against you, but rather us against them."

"Everything you say is one hundred percent on the money. We do up the chances of catching this menace to society. You have no idea how much it pleases me to hear you talk like this, Benny. It's a realistic, grown-up approach to the job. But, since we're getting honest with each other, I have to say I would never have believed those words would be capable of coming out of your mouth. You've apparently grown quite a bit as a law enforcement officer since the last time we worked together. If this new attitude is for real, then I would say you've grown quite a bit as a man also."

Robbins stood there delighted that his little one man play was receiving rave reviews. *This might be easier than I thought*, he anticipated. Time seemed to have dulled Agent Borden's rather keen ability to detect bullshit. Perhaps, on the other hand, Benny was missing the boat on an aspiring acting career. Whatever the reason was did not matter. Robbins' plan was working…or so he thought.

"I'm willing to give you the benefit of the doubt for now, Benny. But I think you should know that I believe talk is cheap. If you truly have done a complete three-sixty, it will show in your actions. I haven't gotten where I am today by judging a book by it's cover. So why don't we get right to work. I haven't eaten. Let's go to the Stir Fry Café, grab a bite to eat and you can start filling me in on everything you have. Remember, the only way I can really help is if you are completely honest with me. Also keep in mind that our window of opportunity for catching this animal has probably gotten smaller with the Feds coming into the picture. That's usually the case. So it would be very beneficial to our cause if I didn't have to retrace your footsteps and try to follow up leads that may have already dried up."

Detective Robbins did his best not to show the wind seeping out of his sails. Apparently, he would not get an Oscar for his perfomance here tonight. He knew he must remain calm and undaunted to keep his charade alive.

"I've got nothing to hide, Sandy. I want this bastard. Period!"

"We'll get him, Benny. I'll tell you what. If you're straight with me, you'll get credit for the collar, and all the accolades that go with it. I could care less about that shit. You'd be the town hero. It might even be enough to get you out from under your cousin's shadow. This is the kind of bust that can make your whole career valid. Know what I mean?"

"Yeah… I know what you mean. That would probably change my life for good. I might even be accepted by my peers for the first time in the twenty three years I've worked for the county. I'll have to admit that sounds too good to be true. Why would you do that for me? What's the catch?"

"No catch. I guess in a way I've always felt a little guilty about the way things ended up for you the last time we worked together. Not for the results, mind you. I still think it was worth letting James off the hook. We made a lot of arrests and confiscated a ton of drugs. But, in retrospect, I realize that you may have ended up with egg on your face. For that, I apologize. It truly wasn't my intention for that to happen."

"Thanks for the apology. My life did take a turn for the worse after that. I hated that James got a free ride. Still do, I suppose." Robbins stopped for a moment to regroup. Suddenly a loud noise went off in his head. This couldn't be happening again. Why was he being nice? What was his angle? What bombshell was about to be dropped by Borden? Robbins decided to take the offensive. "Why are you saying all this to me? Is it because James' name keeps popping up? He's the only suspect I have. Don't tell me you're gonna march right in here and automatically give that son-of-a-bitch a get out of jail free card."

"Slow down, Benny. I'm not saying anything other than I'm sorry for any pain you may have been caused on my part. I know James is the one all the evidence points to. If he's guilty, I guarantee that he goes down hard. What I am saying is that if you tamper with evidence or manipulate this case in any way to settle the score on some personal grudge you have with James, I will personally see to it that your ass goes down. Plain and simple. Remember, I am on your side. But, my first loyalty is to justice being served."

Chapter 54

June 1, 2006

Frank James stood in the middle of the dining room staring out the plate glass window into the parking lot. He was feeling good about the training session he had just held for his staff. Everyone seemed eager to learn exactly how he wanted things done. They picked up the computer that Frank installed as the point of sale system for the deli. It was pretty basic and was fully equipped with "dummy screens" that would not allow you to proceed unless everything was done correctly. The real challenge was learning the layout of the menu screens and the actual closing of guest checks to cash, credit or coupon. Those skills would be strengthened by use of the system.

The physical aspects of the job were such that his employees could either perform them easily or not at all. Frank was confident that, with basic repetition, the staff would perform well above average in all areas. After all, how hard is it to make a sandwich or salad? Menu knowledge was the key and Frank was drilling that into each member of the staff. Each were given copies of the menu to take home and study. There would be a test one week from today on the entire menu. Frank promised a twenty five dollar cash bonus as an incentive to all those who obtained a perfect score on the test. In this day and age, cash seemed to be a sure fire motivator for people of all ages and backgrounds.

As Frank stood there imagining the parking lot full of hungry patrons, he began to feel confident for the first time, since all this madness began, that he would actually be able to open the deli on schedule. That would surely make the investors pleased, considering the worries they had from all the controversy surrounding Frank recently. He had been open and honest with the investors about everything with the hopes that his honesty would stop them from pulling the plug on this whole deal. As of now, they were officially fully supportive of Frank, but he was unsure just how long that would last without some real progress and positive updates.

Frank realized that the confidence he was feeling at this moment needed to be savored. One thing he had learned was that when life gives you cherries, the pits aren't usually too far behind. In this case, Frank's cherries were the hope of a smooth and timely opening of the deli. That being said, the sight of Benny Robbins' Crown Victoria and two Knox County cruisers, with lights ablaze for full effect, pulling into the parking lot was, without a doubt, the pits.

Chapter 55

L ost in the current onslaught of sirens and screeching tires, Frank had forgotten that he was not alone at the deli. As he sensed that he was being watched, he turned slowly to find Marco, Carl Metcalf and his sister, Rose, standing there with mouths agape at the spectacle unfolding before their very own eyes.

Frank didn't want them to see what was about to transpire. He would just as soon take this one on the chin without a crowd. However, he wasn't totally sure that their presence was all bad. He may very well need someone to try to bond him out of jail in the very near future. At the very least, he would need someone to contact his attorney.

There was a quick struggle in Frank's mind between his own pride and common sense. As was the norm, his pride won out. Stubborn pride may be more accurate. Perhaps even foolish pride.

Nonetheless, he turned to his cohorts and conveyed his wishes to them. "I don't want you guys here for this. Carl, take Rose home for me please. Both of you keep the phone lines open in case I'm only allowed one phone call from where I think I'm headed. Maybe one of you could call Brad Covington and alert him to my current situation. The number is in the rolodex on the desk in the office."

Rose spoke up. "Frank, you may need us here. Stop playing the hero. You don't have to go through this on your own."

That brought about a heavy sigh from James. "Look! You all are going to have plenty of time to show your support for me. Right now I need to do this my way. If you really want to help, go home and wait for my call."

Mixed emotions mangled the faces of Rose James and Carl Metcalf. Frustration. Concern. Anger. Even pity. Pity that James felt he had to endure this hell all on his own.

With a silent nod, Carl took hold of Rose's arm and lead her out toward the back door. Metcalf knew all too well that there was no changing Frank's mind once it was set in stone. This seemed to definitely be one of those times.

James turned to Marco. "Slip out the back, Marco. I'm going to need you the most. You're my alibi. I don't want these bastards putting any pressure on you until we have a chance to come up with a game plan. If I get through this today, you and I will meet with Covington and come up with a strategy to handle this mess."

Marco nodded. As much as he wanted to stick around and watch James squirm, he knew that he must do what James requested in order to stay in character. Besides, Marco had to stay focused on the true objective of his plan. That was to watch James fall apart as ten people close to him die in a loud, grotesque manner. The pot of gold at the end of the rainbow being James' own death. He had to play his part. He could not afford to see James rot away in prison. He must pay the ultimate price for what he had done to Diego.

With that in mind, Marco slipped out the back door, leaving James to face the music Detective Robbins was about to play. Although disappointed with the idea of not being able to watch this play out, Marco was still able to find opportunity in the present situation. With the police concentrating their efforts on Frank James, it would be the perfect time to coordinate the next victim's demise with his cronies.

Marco hit speed dial on his Motorola sliver and barked into the mouthpiece "I want everyone at the hotel in twenty minutes! No excuses! No exceptions!"

Chapter 56

Frank James stood frozen, nervously awaiting to see what sort of backwoods justice was about to be handed out by Detective Benny Robbins. He was unsure if the extra men were there to help detain him, or if it was due to the fact Robbins was a chicken shit underneath that tin star. Either way, he decided he must stay on his toes around this ten-toed sloth.

Robbins glided through the door like a gazelle. Normally, he would have burst through the door like a bull in a china shop. It was obvious that this was the swagger of a man who believed he was handed a crucial piece of evidence that no doubt, put him in the driver's seat in regards to his pursuit of the ruination of Frank James.

"You're looking unusually happy today, Benny."

"Feeling unusually happy today, Frankie-boy."

"What happened? Did Hostess come out with a new line of snack cakes?"

Frank grinned. His little one liner was rewarded with both of his desired results. First off, that goofy, little smirk disappeared from Robbins' fat face. Secondly, it sent a chuckle through the ranks of Deputies that Robbins had assembled, perhaps allowing them to be a little sympathetic to Frank's cause.

The red-faced Detective retorted, " You may not be so damn smug after you hear what I have to tell you! I'm so close to pinning this whole murder spree on you I can taste it. You'll be doing your one man stand up routine in front of the inmate population of Folsom Prison. What do you have to say about that, funny man?"

Michael Fiore

"I'd say that anything you think you have on me is total bullshit! You want me so bad you haven't even been doing your job. I bet I've turned up more real evidence than you ever will. You need to get over what happened between us in the past and concentrate on finding the real killer before more innocent people get killed."

Robbins eased toward James until the two men were face to face. Inches separating Robbins and his nemesis. There was a hateful gleam in his eye. The Detective began to speak in a deliberate whisper.

"Let's get two things straight. First of all, there was no need for me to hunt for evidence. I was confident it would be just a matter of time before you slipped up and led me straight to you. You got lucky here in Knoxville, but your true colors showed up in South Carolina. See, you're a fuck up by nature. The killer left a print on the picture that they placed on the O'Callahan's girl's lap. The Feds have already ruled out the possibility that it was her own. They are confident they'll have a match by the end of tomorrow's business day. My gut tells me it's your print."

Robbins paused to let his left-handed accusation go to work on James' psyche. He kept his eyes glued on James, looking for the slightest hint of uncertainty. James' gaze did not waiver. Robbins continued his assault.

"Here's a copy of the photo." Robbins took the picture from his jacket pocket and tortured James with it. "They say a picture is worth a thousand words. I say this picture is priceless because of one word…guilty!"

James kept his cool. "Nice speech, Benny. I'm thinking of one word, too. Circumstantial. Seems like you came here to go fishing, but I'm not taking the bait. You said for me to keep in mind two things. Enlighten me on point number two so you can be on your way."

Since Robbins' attempt at intimidation had fallen on deaf ears, he decided to take a shot below the belt.

"The second thing I wanted to say was that you can quit whining about innocent people dying. Since each of the victims have had some sort of tie to you, I'm sure they were anything but innocent. More than likely, they got what was coming to them."

Blind rage overtook Frank James. Without thinking, he clenched his fists and began to lunge after Robbins. He knew he was playing right into Robbins' hand, but was unable to control his fury. Robbins prepared himself to accept a blow from James in order to have him arrested on the spot. To Robbins' surprise, however, two Deputies raced between the two men, encouraging Frank not to let Robbins win. They pushed him back, holding on until his rage subsided.

Furious, Robbins barked at the two officers. "You sorry sons-a-bitches! You can bet the Sheriff will hear about this!"

One of the thick, barrel-chested Deputies turned to Robbins and snapped back. "You're a no good piece of shit, Benny. Go cry to your cousin. He knows what an asshole you are. But you better get outta here fast, or we may just let this guy have a whack at you."

Robbins, sensing he was now outnumbered, decided a quick retreat was in order. He waddled his way to the front door. Unable to leave without getting the last word in, he turned to James and said, "If I were you, I'd go out tonight, have a nice, fat steak and get you a little piece of ass. I'll be back tomorrow with competent, loyal backup to haul your ass in!"

With that, Robbins about-faced, disappeared into his Crown Vic and took off like a shot out of the parking lot, leaving Frank James disoriented and uncertain about exactly how much time he had left as a free man.

Chapter 57

Miguel Escobar stood in front of his troops, giddy with anticipation of the demise of their next target. Once he had their undivided attention, he began to tell them the name of the next victim and exactly how and when he wanted them to perform their duties.

Javier rose and began, hesitantly, to speak. "Jefe, I don't understand why we go after this Metcalf guy. He lives right here in Knoxville. The whole town is crawling with locals looking for us. And now with the Feds coming in…"

Miguel cut him off with simple raising of his hand. He glared at Javier and in a hushed tone grumbled, "Are you questioning me, Javier?"

"No, Jefe, it's just…"

"Sounds to me like you were questioning me and now you are interrupting me as well. Answer me this. Who's in charge here?"

"You are. I'm not disputing that. It justs seems very risky right now. Maybe we should lay low a bit. We've worked very hard for you. No questions asked. We could use a little break. That's all. Hit the club again. Remember how much fun that was?"

"You've been paid well to do the work I've asked of you. You've not been paid to think or question my methods. Not to offer your opinions or suggestions either, for that matter!"

Miguel paced back and forth until he came to a halt in front of Javier, rubbing his temples momentarily. In one fluid motion, he drew his 9mm from his belt and placed the barrel firmly against his cohort's temple.

"When you question me...I question your loyalty. When I have to question your loyalty...someone dies! Is that clear enough?"

Javier apologized with sweat rolling off his brow. He had underestimated the ruthlessness of this man he thought of as a friend.

"I'm very sorry, Jefe. I meant no disrespect. You have no reason to question my loyalty. I guess I just need to blow off some steam. This will never happen again. Please give me another chance. Por favor, Jefe."

"Very well. Just do as I ask. One more thing. No one leaves this room for any reason other than to perform their assigned tasks. We cannot afford to be seen. No dinner, no drinks and certainly no clubs! If there's no other questions, I must go to meet Rose James at Ruby Tuesday's. Do not vary from the plan."

Sandoval waited to be sure Escobar would not return. He peeked through the curtains and glanced in both directions before turning to his two friends sitting quietly on the bed.

"What the hell are you two moping for? You're not actually afraid of him are you?"

Tranquillo spoke up. "We are not afraid of anything. We just wanted to go out and have some fun."

"So go! You heard him. He's on his way to some restaurant to enjoy himself. Why should he have all the fun when it is you that is doing all of the dirty work?"

Javier and Troncillo looked confused that Escobar's best friend would have them go against their boss' wishes. Before they could accuse him of anything, Sandoval turned the tables on them.

"Look, I'm not telling you that you shouldn't take this guy out. By all means, do it. When you're through, go out and enjoy yourselves. What Miguel doesn't know won't hurt him. Besides, I will smooth everything over with him if he even suspects that we disobeyed him."

Sandoval was amazed at how little it took to sway those two into this seemingly minor rebellion that would prove monumental in his own personal cause. The potential sacrifice of his friends seemed of little consequence. After all, it was Miguel himself who had always told him that sometimes there were necessary casualties in order to keep your eye on the prize.

Chapter 58

F rank James pulled into the driveway of his apartment on Indiana
Avenue. His mind was still reeling from the day's events. He had
spent the last ninety minutes being assured by Brad Covington that
there was no way they could detain him for any length of time. Even
if Detective Robbins made good on his threat to arrest James the
following day. All the assurance in the world wasn't going to change
the fact that, within the next twenty four hours, James could lose his
freedom, his deli and a shot at reconciliation with the only woman he
had ever truly loved.

The thought of jail and the chance of not being able to realize his
dream of the Knuckle Sandwich Deli were enough to make James
sick to his stomach. The thought of losing Tina after all this time,
however, brought back an anger that he had not experienced for
some time. He truly believed his sanity would not remain intact if the
walls came crumbling down around him.

While Frank was unsure what the following day would bring
him, he was positive of what his next move should be. He had to call
Tina. They had to get together tonight. There was no way he could
risk being arrested tomorrow without being able to profess his love
for her one last time. More so, he would have to make her believe he
was innocent. No small task. Considering his past and the lies that
used to run his life, it would be just short of miraculous to get her to
believe.

After a hot, relaxing shower, James got dressed and prepared
himself to call Tina. He kept hearing Robbins' last words. *'Go out,*

have a nice, fat steak and get you a little piece of ass. I'll be back tomorrow to haul your ass in!' He found it humorous that he would ever follow advice given to him by the obnoxiously obese Detective obsessed with ruining his life. But, here he was about to do that very thing.

Frank took a deep breath and dialed Tina's number. It rang. Once. Twice. Thrice. *Oh, damn!,* Frank thought. What a horrible little joke life would play on him if he weren't able to get in touch with this woman.

The fourth ring. With it, came fear. Fear of being alone for his 'Last Supper.'

The fifth ring. With it came disappointment. Tina would have to hear the news of Frank's arrest on television.

Ring number six. Next came despair. He would never be able to touch her face or feel her kiss ever again.

With the seventh ring came…

"Hello?"

Oh, the humanity of it all. Her voice was as beautiful a thing as he had ever heard.

"Hey, baby. It's Frank."

"You've got great timing. I was in the shower. Too bad you don't have phone-a-vision, because I'm in my birthday suit dripping all over the kitchen floor."

Frank's whole body came alive. All he could picture was this gorgeous creature standing there in all her glory. *Benny who?* Frank smiled.

"Listen, Tina. There's a bunch going on that I wanted you to hear about from me. I was hoping you'd let me take you to dinner tonight and fill you in. Whadda ya say?"

"Sorry, babe. I've got a work thing. I absolutely have to show up. Can't we do it tomorrow?"

There was a long hesitation by Frank. Deep down he didn't think tomorrow was an option. He tried his best not to let his desparation come through in his voice.

"Um…yeah…maybe we can. Sorry to bother you. I'll let you get ready. Bye."

"Wait! Frank! What's wrong?"

"Nothin'. It can wait."

"Listen, I don't know what makes you think that you can bullshit me. I believe I've both earned and deserve the truth. So quit you're freakin' whining and spill the beans!"

Frank had to laugh out loud. There was definitely no getting anything over on her. She was right about deserving the truth, as well. Out of love and respect, Frank filled her in on all the details of the day's events, as well as what tomorrow most likely had in store for him.

Tina listened earnestly. When Frank was finished, she asked if she could tell him something. Frank waited for her to unleash a fury spawned from Hell and aimed directly at him. What he got was totally different from what he expected. There was nothing Frank would have rather heard than the three simple words that came from Tina's lips.

"I believe you."

Frank was stunned. He needed to hear those words. They somehow made everything that was happening seem to not matter so much. He was close to being speechless and barely managed to utter a simple thank you.

Tina thought for a moment and said, "Frank, I really have to go to this dinner. But, I'll tell you what. Be here around ten o'clock. I'd love to see you tonight. Besides, maybe I'd better give you your birthday present in case you're not available on the sixth. How does that sound?"

Frank choked back the tears.

"That sounds terrific. I'll be there."

"Oh, yeah. One more thing, Frank."

"What is it?"

"I love you."

At that moment, Frank realized it would take an entire army of Benny Robbins' to keep him away from this incredible woman. Hope filled him. His faith reappeared, too. In an instant, all of his hard work over the last three years had become validated.

"I love you, too. See you at ten."

Chapter 59

James found himself pacing uncontrollably throughout his entire apartment. He stopped to look at the clock on the microwave. Six fifteen. These next three and a half hours would seem like an eternity while he waited for his rendezvous with Tina.

He looked around for any little chores that might help him shave some time off of, what seemed to Frank, like being on house arrest. The fact that he hadn't spent much time at home over the last week made it difficult. There really wasn't anything that needed the slightest bit of tidying up.

Frank sat down and opened up the latest James Patterson novel. Surely that would help eat some time off the clock. After scanning the same paragraph for the third time, Frank realized that he was unable to focus on anything but his long awaited date with the woman he loved.

He glanced at the clock on the mantle. Seven o'clock. This was excruciating. But, oh how the anticipation was bringing to life every single molecule in his body. Frank tilted his head back and closed his eyes in order to visualize one possible scenario that, God willing, could have a chance at becoming reality later on this evening.

In his mind, Frank slowly approached the gazeebo in Tina's backyard. An aromatic path of freshly plucked rose petals had led him to what turned out to be a Heavenly vision. In the center of the gazeebo stood his saucy little vixen in an ultra sheer white teddy. A rather robust evening breeze had it's way with Tina's silky locks. The moonlight hit her from behind, giving her an incredibly sensual luminescence that made it impossible for his Levi's to conceal Frank's raw animal appreciation for her choice of attire, as well as the backdrop she had chosen to unleash the lingerie's full effect.

Pulling this luscious morsel close to him, Frank gently tugged at her hair to slightly tilt her head to one side. His face moving closer to hers ever so slowly. Their eyes fastened intently on each others. Tina parted her lips and Frank began to descend upon them to quench this passion that had been building up inside for three long years. Just as their lips brushed together…KNOCK! KNOCK!

Frank opened up his eyes in disbelief. *Who in the hell could this be*, he wondered. Whoever it was would surely not receive a very hearty welcome. Not after interrupting the steamy little daydream he had concocted.

James got up off the couch, flattening out the bulge that had stemmed from the scenario he had just developed in his mind.

KNOCK! KNOCK!

"Hold on. I'm coming."

There was no way in a million years that Frank James could have been prepared for who was on the other side of that threshold. He turned the knob and pulled open the door. Frank stood in amazement, with his jaw touching the floor. For the second time tonight he was speechless.

"Hey, Frank. Long time no see."

There was no response.

"Frank, can I come in?"

"Um, yeah. Come in."

It had been several years since he had seen Agent Sandy Borden. Despite his surprised look and the mild shock he felt, Frank knew in an instant the odds of him getting a fair shake had just increased dramatically.

Chapter 60

Agent Sandy Borden sat at the kitchen table sipping on black coffee while James cracked open his usual can of coke. If it weren't for the fact that Borden was there in an official capacity, one might have thought it was merely two friends catching up on old times. While the term 'friends' may not be quite accurate, there had always been a mutual respect between the two men that could have easily cultivated into friendship.

Borden noticed the look of uncertainty plastered across James' face. He saw no reason to make Frank sweat anymore than he already had. Borden placed his cup on the table, looked James in the eyes and said, "I imagine you're wondering what the hell I'm doing here?"

Frank managed a weak smile.

"The thought had crossed my mind."

"Well then, let's cut to the chase. Once they found the O'Callahan girl's body in South Carolina, the FBI got the green light to take over the lead on the case. When they learned that Robbins was in charge and you were the first, and only, name on his hit parade, their decision on who to bring in got real easy. The big wigs thought I was the obvious choice because of my past association with the both of you."

Frank's surprise wasn't that Borden was sent to Knoxville to take over. It was the fact that he showed up at his apartment, alone, at this time of the evening. Borden continued as if he read Frank's mind.

"The only reason I'm here right now is really very simple. Since

I've arrived here in Knoxville, all of my information has been coming from basically one source. That source being Benny Robbins. While I'm sure the case that he's building is somewhat based on fact, or at least what he believes to be fact, I wouldn't have been able to get where I'm at today if I didn't explore all possible angles of every investigation. In this case, I figured I needed to hear your side of the story. So let's have it."

"My side? That's easy. I'm innocent."

Borden smiled.

"Can you elaborate. I mean, there seems to be quite a bit of evidence pointing at you."

James could feel his blood begin to boil.

"Evidence? More like coincidence. Look, I've been cooperating with this investigation from the get go. Hell, I hand delivered this so called evidence to Benny for Christ's sake. Why would I do that if I was guilty?"

Borden responded in his usual stoic fashion.

"Popular opinion is that you did it to throw the dogs off the scent."

"Look! I've come too far to throw it all away by feeling the need to start killing people. Besides, these victims were friends of mine. It's all been so random. There's no motive. Not to mention the fact that I haven't been to South Carolina in years. A fact which makes it awful hard for me to have been in Greenville when Allison was killed. There's also a little thing called an alibi for the time I was supposed to be spreading my murder spree across state lines."

Borden scowled.

"This is the first time I've heard anything about an alibi."

"I'm sure there's a lot you haven't heard about. Nobody seems to care about listening to the facts."

"Well, I'm here right now. Tell me everything you know. If it's not you, who is it?"

Frank took a deep breath. He knew in his heart that this was the only chance to explain his theory of what was happening. Borden would surely hear him out. It was up to him to make his story believable. He got up and began pacing back and forth in front of agent Borden.

"Okay. Here goes. I think someone is trying to set me up to take the fall. I don't know who or why exactly, but they are choosing people that are, or were, close to me at one time or another. Our pasts are what makes it easy for them to leave clues implicating me."

"Is that a theory or paranoia?"

At that moment, a very important piece of the puzzle that Frank had been overlooking made itself apparent. He paused. His thinking suddenly became as clear as a bell.

"About a week or so ago, I was on my way to tell my friend Mark that I had gotten the backing for my new deli. I got the feeling that someone was following me. When I got to Cumberland Avenue, I did some fancy maneuvering in traffic and made a quick turn onto Seventeenth Street. When I looked back, there was a black Cadillac Escalade with Florida plates that came to a screeching halt. There were two Hispanic looking guys inside. The one driving looked me dead in the eyes and pounded on the steering wheel."

Borden's curiosity was beginning to peak. *Where could this be going*, he thought. Maybe he could help steer James in the right direction.

"Why do you think they could possibly have anything to do with you being set up?"

Frank's face started to glow. It all started to make sense.

"I talked to the bouncer, Travis, at the club where Sam worked. He said that she left with four high rollers the night she was killed. Hispanic high rollers."

"That could be considered coincidence as well. Don't you think?"

"But there's more. The night Johnny was killed. Kristy, the bartender at Spicy's, told me that Johnny was getting pretty friendly with two Hispanic strangers. The three men left together."

This was getting good. Borden had to admit that this was beginning to seem very possible. There were, however, a few more questions still left unanswered.

"What about the O'Callahan murder?"

Frank stopped Borden in his tracks. "Look. I bet if you sent someone to the Corner Pocket in Greenville, someone there would tell you there were a couple of Hispanic strangers that became real friendly with Allison the day she died. Can you atleast have someone check it out? Tell them you're following a hunch."

Agent Borden, forever playing the devil's advocate, decided to strike a deal with James.

"If you can give me an explanation about the picture we found on her body, I'll check out your theory. But I have to tell you Frank, they found a print. It's yours. I wasn't going to let that information out until I spoke with you."

Frank's mouth went dry. He had no explanation. He remembered the photo that Robbins had shown him earlier in the day.

"Sandy, all I can tell you is that I have no idea how my print got on the photo. In all honesty, I have that same picture in a frame in the living room."

Frank headed into the living room with Agent Borden hot on his heels. When he got to where he left the picture, he stopped dead in his tracks. He slowly turned to Borden holding an empty, broken frame.

"I think I can explain my fingerprint on that picture. It's my picture."

Borden stood a moment with his mouth agape. Everything in him believed that they were finally on the right track.

"Sold! I'll get someone down to the Corner Pocket ASAP! I'll be in touch."

Chapter 61

While it appeared as though Frank would spend an eternity waiting for the hands on the clock to strike ten, thanks to Agent Sandy Borden's impromptu visit, the magical hour arrived in what seemed like the blink of an eye. He could feel an unimaginable energy surging through his entire body as he pulled the Concorde in front of Tina's house. Partly due to his anticipation of tonight's reunion with his lost love. Partly due to the result of his very enlightening meeting with the agent leading the FBI's investigation of the so-called Headless Horseman killings.

Frank found himself climbing the porch steps, just as he had done a thousand times before. However, this time was completely different. Never before had his heart raced this much. His brow broke out in a cold sweat. What Frank believed to be anticipation and excitement on the ride over had, in an instant, turned to anxiety and stress.

"This is crazy! I've been waiting almost three years for this very moment. Why am I...why am I talking to myself for God's sake."

James took a deep breath and held it for a moment. He let it out ever so slowly, trying to clear his thoughts. He decided there was nothing to fear. This was his destiny. He would not allow anything to keep him from his destiny.

Straightening his clothes one last time, Frank reached out and began tapping on the front door. He heard Tina's melodic voice grant him entrance to her castle. What came next was beyond Frank's wildest dreams.

The door creaked as Frank slowly pushed it open. He stood at the threshold, stunned, as he stared into the living room. It was illuminated by what Frank thought to be dozens of vanilla scented candles of all shapes and sizes. As he scanned the room, his attention was drawn to a path of scantily scattered sun flower petals leading through the maze of candles and ending at the circular staircase that ascended to a loft that had been converted into the master bedroom.

Whatever calm Frank was able to restore before knocking was instantly erased as he began to navigate the fragrant path that, most assuredly, would lead him to his idea of the promise land.

James' pulse was revving well into the red by the time he reached the top of the staircase. Several more candles gave the room a soft, sensual glow.

Out of the corner of his eye, James spotted his prey. Posing ever so sexy in the doorway to the bathroom was a silhouette outlined perfectly by a sheer, red silk teddy. It was, in fact, the same teddy that Frank had bought for her the last Valentine's Day they had shared before the break up. The effect it had on Frank was even greater than the first time. He chalked that up to the three years he had spent longing for this beautiful woman.

"You look amazing. I need to pinch myself to make sure I'm not dreaming."

Tina gave her best crooked smile.

"It's real alright. Baby, it's all for you. I've missed you so much."

The two met in a passionate embrace. Their lips pressing together. Gently at first. Then, with a hunger so fierce, it unlocked a raw, animal passion that would leave these lovers devouring each other for hours in order for the fire to be extinguished. A fire that had been smouldering the last three years, just aching for this chance to burst out of control.

Tina's fingers fumbled with the buttons on Frank's shirt to no avail. She couldn't see what she was doing because she did not want to end this embrace. Frustrated, she finally took a step back from Frank. With one eyebrow raised, she began inspecting the clothing that was between her and her lover, looking for the fastest way to peel it off. With a devilish smile and a slight lick of the lips, she reached out and tore Frank's shirt from his trembling body. Buttons flying everywhere.

She dug her nails gently into his freshly shaved chest, outlining his surprisingly well defined pecs. *He's done some working out over the last three years*, Tina thought. Next, she began to leave a trail of soft, wet kisses on Frank's torso, beginning at his neck, just below his ear, descending ever so slowly. Her lips reached his chest. She flicked her tongue playfully over his nipples and continued south.

As she reached his belly button, Tina hesitated, glanced up and gave James a wide-eyed, nasty little smile as she initiated her assault on his blue jeans. She looked like a kid at Christmas, eagerly anticipating her best gift yet.

Frank stepped out of his jeans and pulled Tina off her knees, turning her body so that she was facing away from him. He swept her silky locks away from her ear as he began to nibble on her neck and shoulders. All the while, his eager hands leaving her velvety flesh ablaze from their gentle caress.

The couple's hunger reached it's climax as the two became one, collapsing, exhausted atop the sweat stained sheets on Tina's bed. Gazing intently into each others eyes, the reunited duo pledged their undying devotion to one another without a single word.

Chapter 62

June 2, 2006

Frank was awakened by a choir of birds that had assembled outside the bedroom window. He immediately looked beside him to assure himself that he had not been dreaming. That the romantic interlude of a lifetime had, in fact, been real.

There was Tina lying next to him. Her soft and toasty naked body melting into his, making it virtually impossible to tell where her body ended and his began. The birds had not interrupted her slumber. She lay there almost purring with contentment. As usual, it would have taken a marching band to make her bat an eye before she was ready.

Frank glanced over at the clock on the end table. Six thirty in the morning. He hated that this had to end so soon, but he had to make arrangements for things to get done, should he be arrested by the bumbling oaf of a detective that was out for his hide.

He leaned over and laid a soft, lingering kiss on Tina's temple, gently brushing the hair away from her face. God she was beautiful. Frank knew right then and there that he had to face whatever demons that had come back to haunt him. He had to meet them head on and defeat them once and for all, allowing the rest of his mornings to be like this one. Even more so, he needed to put an end to this madness in order to keep Tina out of danger.

James slipped out of bed and into the kitchen. He whipped up a quick continental breakfast that consisted of a cinnamon raisin bagel, half grapefruit and a glass of orange juice without pulp. He placed the items on a tray and lightly decorated it with the same sun flower petals from the night before.

He made his way back to the bedroom only to find Tina no longer in bed. So much for a little romantic surprise breakfast in bed. He placed the tray on the bed and began to gather his clothes.

Tina made her way out of the bathroom.

"What do we have here? Ooh, breakfast. If I'd have known, I would have stayed in bed. I woke up, saw you were gone and figured you crawled away in shame, unable to face me this morning. I felt so cheap!"

Nothing like a little morning sarcasm to get your day started off on the right foot. Frank smiled.

"You didn't think for one damn minute I'd leave without telling you how much I love you. Besides, I'm still waiting for my birthday present."

"I'm afraid you unwrapped that last night. Sorry it looks a little scarier this morning than it did when you first opened it."

Frank pulled her tight, kissed her lips and said, "It looks every bit as amazing as it did last night. Don't kid yourself."

"Then why are you looking like you're about to leave?"

"Come on, baby. I'm not sure how much time I have today. You can bet your ass that Robbins will be coming after me today. I need some time to make arrangements before that happens. I need to call Brad Covington. I need to have Marco open the deli and let the staff use the computers. Most of all, I want to make sure that he doesn't show up here and cause a scene. I don't want you to witness this."

Tina looked confused.

"I thought you said the FBI was on your side? Doesn't that mean you can tell that fat bastard to go to Hell?"

"I'm sure Agent Borden won't let me sit in jail for long, but if Robbins can get to me first, he can make it a pretty rough day for me. I need to try and stay a step ahead of that worthless piece of shit."

"Where does that leave me? Don't you think I'll be worrying my ass off until I hear from you?"

"It would take an awful lot of worry to worry that ass off."

Tina scowled at Frank's attempt at humor. She knew he was just trying to lighten up the situation, but she still wanted to slap him.

"Look, baby. I'll stay in touch. You'll be the first to know if anything happens. That's the best I can do."

She pouted.

"Well, that sucks!"

Frank grabbed Tina's face with both hands, kissing her gently on the mouth.

"Listen, nobody, but nobody is going to keep me from you. I promise everything is going to be alright."

With that, James gave her one final peck on the cheek and headed out the door. As much as Tina wanted to believe, the history of bad luck and disappointment when dealing with Frank James left her extremely pessimistic that things would, in fact, be alright.

Chapter 63

Frank James could feel the paranoia building with every rotation of the tires as he made his way home from Tina's house. His knuckles turned white as he held onto the steering wheel with all his might. His eyes constantly scanning his perimeter, waiting for sirens and blue lights to rain down on him like something out of a bad Japanese science fiction movie.

James wondered how he could have pissed off God enough to let such an insignificant S.O.B. like Benny Robbins have so much power over him. The very thought of him took Frank out of his game. All of the hard work to become a strong, confident, clean member of society. Was all that work merely a ruse? It appeared as such to James for the first time as he made his way back to his apartment in Maryville.

"What am I doing?!", Frank exclaimed aloud, letting go of the wheel long enough to pound his fists against it. All his life he let every little set back chip away at his resolve, never allowing himself to reach his full potential. At this moment, he could feel himself giving in just as he had done a thousand times before. The mere thought of giving in to this type of weak thinking was enough to turn his stomach.

Glancing at the pathetic look on his face in the rear view mirror was the last straw. It was time to make a stand. Time to stop cowering. As much as it pissed Frank off, he heard the one line his father used to drill into him no matter what the situation. How he hated to hear that one damn phrase. "Pull yourself up by the bootstraps and be a man!"

Saying it out loud made Frank cringe. It conjured up a hundred different memories of him and his father. None of them very endearing. Frank hadn't had these type of memories come back at him since he and his father had reconciled their differences a few years back. Well, this time, that tough, old bastard would be exactly right to say it to his son.

Frank smiled. Pull himself up was exactly what he would do. The time for whining was over. Right then he decided that he was the one with all the power. Not Benny! He also was determined to let Robbins know that the next time they met face to face.

Frank sat up straight. His chest puffing out ever so slightly. For the first time today, he realized what a magnificent spring day was unfolding before his very own eyes. He was in charge. Besides, he remembered he had something very important going for him…the truth. And, the truth would surely set him free.

Frank whipped his car onto Indiana Avenue with a brand new attitude. He suddenly felt ten feet tall and bulletproof, ready to take whatever Benny Robbins had to dish out. His newfound smugness lasted all of five minutes, however, as his eyes became glued to the half dozen squad cars lining the street in front of his home.

"The truth," Frank said once again. It was then that it became clear to James that the truth had sent many an innocent man away to rot for crimes they had not committed. Yes, the truth sometimes needed an accomplice.

Thank God for Agent Sandy Borden of the FBI. Frank James accomplice in the search for truth.

Chapter 64

I t was business as usual for Carl Metcalf. Up at 6:30AM, cup of strong, black coffee and he was off for his five mile run. The run had become a ritual after a routine doctor's visit had detected a slight cholesterol problem. A healthy diet and exercise was recommended to combat the issue. Since Metcalf wasn't about to give up the red meat and sausages that were part of his daily caloric intake, he opted for a regimen of strenuous exercise that included the morning run, as well as a twenty minute pilates tape he had purchased at Wal-Mart.

Metcalf began two months earlier. What started out as a two mile jaunt had already progressed to a five mile juggernaut. His route was the same each and every day in order to accurately gage his distance. He had dismissed several attempts by his loving wife to convince him to change his route in order to keep the run interesting. Metcalf retorted by insisting that, in order for something to become routine, it had to be just that…routine. They both knew the real reason was that Carl was extremely resistant to change. This character trait was developed back in his IRA days, where it was necessary for survival. Survival. Metcalf would surely come to see the irony in something routine being necessary for survival as his day unfolded.

After his coffee was gone, Metcalf gave his wife a smooch on the cheek and was out the door. He made his way down the front walk stretching and hit the driveway to begin his warm up. Metcalf cracked a smile as he approached the mailbox at the end of his driveway. Pacing anxiously, with his tail in full swing, was his faithful Irish Setter, Flanagan. Flanagan had also made this run a ritual in his own daily life. Carl loved the comraderie offered by his faithful companion.

The two took off down the street, Flanagan jumping out to his usual lead. His youth and speed allowed the canine to combine a morning run with some much needed exploration. He would run ahead anywhere form thirty to fifty yards, then jump in and out of the woods, giving his snout a good workout as well. Metcalf would catch up, the two would run side by side for a moment, then Flanagan would dart out ahead once again. This pattern would go on throughout the entire run.

Metcalf glanced at his watch as he passed the Jennings farm. This was the three mile marker on his journey. Twenty minutes had elapsed since he began. He was making exceptionally good time today. The next mile would determine if he would set a new personal best. The better part of the next mile was uphill and lined on both sides by fairly dense wooded areas. No doubt the steepest and most secluded portion of Metcalf's run.

Fatigue and muscle spasms began to bombard Metcalf as he struggled to reach the apex of this hill that had become his nemesis. It wasn't the pain, however, that was on the forefront of his thoughts. Concern was more like it. He realized that it had been an abnormally long time since he had seen his dog.

Metcalf came to a stop atop the hill and searched in all directions for Flanagan. It wasn't like the dog to desert his master. When his breathing returned to a normal pace, Carl put his fingers to his mouth and let out a piercing whistle.

Nothing.

"Flanagan," he shouted. Still no sign of the pooch. With his hands on his hips, Metcalf wondered if it were possible that his partner may have been in a hurry to get home. It didn't seem likely, but it was possible.

"Flanagan. Here, boy."

Just as Metcalf resigned himself to the fact that he would finish the run on his own, he heard a disheartening yelp from the woods to the left. He headed in the direction of the noise, hoping to hear another distress call from his mutt. Metcalf began to worry as he spotted a light trail of blood on the branches of the evergreens to his right.

"Flanagan. Don't worry. I'm coming, boy."

Metcalf's worry turned to heartache as he spotted his dog in an opening in the trees. He was laying in a heap, perfectly still. As he leaned down to tend to his trusty sidekick, his heartache turned to fear. There was a small caliber bullet hole in the dog's torso, directly behind his right, front leg. The shot was no mistake. But why? Who? Who would do such a thing? Carl knew these questions would never be answered as the chainsaw came to life right behind him.

He had just enough time to say a quick prayer for his wife and give Flanagan one last pat on the head before he felt the burning pain in his neck, causing his world to go black once and for all.

Chapter 65

Frank James had barely gotten the keys out of the ignition as he was swarmed by legions of both uniformed and plain clothes Deputies. Benny Robbins had left nothing to chance. He must have called in every chit he had out there to get this type of turnout. The news of Frank's fingerprint most assuredly had been disclosed by the FBI. Frank could see it in the face of every law enforcement officer at the scene. The hatred. The fear. Many of them just itching to put James out of his misery.

Uncertainty clouded James' mind. He was uncertain what his next move should be. Uncertain what Robbins' unruly mob would do. But most of all, he was uncertain why he was even in this predicament to begin with. Who could he have hurt so badly that made them want him to take the fall for these murders.

A familiar face appeared amidst the throngs of police issued 9mm's, sniper rifles and shotguns. Benny Robbins. Just one glance at his smug face made it easy to see he was in all his glory. He paraded around the front of Frank's car and raised a bull horn to his lips.

"Get out of the car with your hands up. If you make one false move, I promise you I'll let these good 'ole boys use you for target practice. Ya see, we don't take kindly to killers in these here parts."

Frank's body seemed frozen in place in the front seat of his Concorde. He heard Benny's command. His brain sent the message to his extremities. They simply could not respond. Funny how staring down the barrel of a gun made even the most simple of movements quite complicated.

"I know you can hear me, James! Get your ass out of the car...NOW!"

As the numbness slowly left James' body, he put both hands out the window, opening the car door with his left hand. As the door swung open, James gently slid his legs out of the driver's seat. By the time his heels hit the pavement, he was swarmed by a half dozen officers.

James couldn't count the number of hands responsible for jerking him out of his vehicle and slamming him to the blacktop. Once he was eating gravel, several knees violently introduced themselves to James' torso. One at the base of his neck, with two more viciously planted on his spine. One at the middle and the other at the base of his back.

Frank tried to relax his body to absorb the blows. He knew full well that any type of resistance, including trying to defend himself, would give Robbins and his crew all the excuse they needed to cause some real physical damage. Excruciating pain surged through his back and shoulders as his arms were nearly pulled out of the sockets in order to apply the handcuffs.

Robbins stood by, thoroughly enjoying the punishment being dealt to James. He loved to see him grimace in pain. Benny would have preferred to see a bit more blood than was trickling out of Frank's nose, but found himself content with the multitude of cheap shots James was being pelted with by the officers.

On Detective Robbins' cue, the beating stopped and James was yanked to his feet. His bruised and slightly bloodied face most definitely gave Robbins a cheap thrill. How Frank despised that arrogant bastard. He stood there ready to bite his tongue and not show any type of response to the verbal assault that the pig of a Detective was about to unleash on him. Talk about a captive audience.

"What's wrong, Frankie-boy? No more jokes? If you ask me, this is the funniest I've ever seen you."

James tried to avoid making eye contact with Robbins. He stood there staring at his shoes, trying to concentrate on anything other than what was transpiring before him. Frank was brought back to reality suddenly, as one of Benny's meat hooks slammed into the side of his face.

"I told you I'd be back to get you, you murdering son-of-a-bitch. It pleases me to no end to be the one to bring you in. The only thing that would make me happier would be flipping the switch and being able to smell your burning flesh as you fry before my eyes."

"Have your fun now, Benny. You don't have shit on me."

"The fingerprint came back. It's yours. That makes you a murderer."

"Fuck you and your fingerprint, you filthy scumbag. All you did here today is bring on a lawsuit against Knox County. And, if there is a God, cost yourself your job. So, get you a few more good shots in while you have all these rednecks here to back you up. But let me assure you right here and now, there will come a time when it's just you and me. I guarantee I won't forget this and will repay you ten times over."

"Is that a threat, tough guy?"

"A promise, you worthless piece of shit."

"We shall see, Frankie-boy, we shall see."

Robbins motioned to his flunkies.

"Put his ass in the car and take him downtown. I'm sick of the sight of him."

As the patrol car rolled away from Indiana Avenue, Frank couldn't help but wonder how long it would take Sandy Borden to get wind of this and come to his rescue. He hoped it would be soon. Everything in his body told him that if he was put into the population of Knox County Jail, there was a very good chance he would not make it out alive.

Chapter 66

Frank's mind was spinning out of control. He was trying to make some kind of sense out of the events that had transpired since Sam's death. This whole scenario seemed somewhat surreal to James. Well, it seemed surreal up to this moment. What was happening now was very real. Not only real, but frighteningly disturbing.

Sitting in the fetal position, with his arms clamped tightly behind his back, brought James back to a time in his life that he would have just as soon forgot. The familiar smell of urine and tobacco that filled the back of the squad car was enough to make him gag. Never in a million years would he have expected to be in the back of another police cruiser on his way to jail once again. Not since he had been clean, anyway.

James was handed another dose of reality as the car approached the gate to the County Jail. The expressionless guard manning the gate motioned the vehicle through. James cringed as an unnerving humming sound began, signaling the closing of the barb-wire rimmed stockade behind him. Once that humming stopped, there was no going back. James closed his eyes and rattled off a quick prayer to his Maker, hoping that he would not become a casualty in this backward, redneck hell.

The patrol car slid to a stop in front of a single iron door dwarfed by a huge façade of concrete and brick. The two beefy Deputies assigned to escort James in got out of the car and stood guard, patiently awaiting for the lead Detective to arrive and take the prisoner through the booking process.

As Robbins' Crown Victoria pulled into the bay next to their patrol car, the two Deputies opened the back door and yanked James out of the car. Robbins dismissed his men and pushed the call button on the intercom. He showed his credentials to the camera. The intake officer pressed a button unlatching the door, allowing Robbins and James to enter into a small foyer. Once inside, the outer door electronically slammed shut.

Here James was forced to remove all personal items, as well as his socks, shoes and belt. Once these items were placed in a mesh bag and slid through what resembled a drive-thru window at a bank, Robbins began a thorough search. Satisfied that James had no contraband on his person, Robbins attached leg irons and James was brought into the main intake area.

The intake area consisted of a large, rectangular desk in the center of the room. Single person cells lined the wall to the left of the desk, while larger, group holding cells lined the wall to the right. Each cell in full view of the guards behind the desk. A stainless steel bench faced the front of the desk and was used to detain prisoners awaiting transportation to a number of destinations, as well as prospective inmates waiting to make their one phone call.

The booking process was normally a long, drawn out affair, taking anywhere from two to six hours, depending on the competence and diligence of the officers on duty. Although this was normally a grueling time for prisoners, James was hoping that his particular booking would take as long as possible. The more time he spent in intake, the more likely he would be rescued prior to being put in population.

James was placed in a solitary cell, his shackles removed, and was left to sit on a small cement slab that served as both bench and cot to the inmates. A stainless steel, seatless toilet completed the décor. He was offered no pillow, no blanket and no food. This treatment was the norm for any inmate the jailers wanted to try and break. Usually the hardened criminals, which James was being looked upon as.

After nearly forty-five minutes, Frank's cell was opened and his presence was requested at the front desk. The shift sergeant completed all of the necessary paperwork, Frank's prints were taken and he was dressed out in an orange Knox County jumpsuit. Robbins remained for the entire process, taunting James throughout. This was, no doubt, the single, most wonderful day of his career in law enforcement.

With his booking complete, Frank was brought out once more. All eyes were on him and Detective Robbins. With a huge smile on his face, Robbins pushed James up against the wall with all his might.

"I've been waiting for this day for quite some time, you miserable excuse for a human being. You've become sort of an obsession for me ever since you got away clean the last time we were together. You gave me friggin' nightmares. You made my life a living hell."

Franked smiled.

"Glad I could help, Benny."

Robbins' face turned beet red. He lunged forward, ready to smash James' head against the wall. The desk sergeant called out to Robbins' attention the video camera directly above his head. Benny stopped, straightened his tie and laughed.

"See! See how you get me going! Well, I don't need to do anything more to you. Once you head through those doors, you're destined to rot away in some prison until we get the death penalty. You'll never taste freedom again. What do you have to say about that, wise ass?"

"I'd say that you give a real nice speech. Very intimidating. Christ, I'm shaking."

Frank smiled from ear to ear. Pointing to the door he had entered from not long ago, he went on to finish his own little speech.

"I'd also say that you were a bit premature. As usual. I don't think I'm going anywhere but home."

Robbins snorted at Frank's tenacity.

"You've got some balls, James. I'll give you that. But, those balls aren't gonna be enough to get you out of here. So, please, tell me how you plan to leave here. I'm sure everyone is just dying to know."

"I'm gonna leave here with a friend of mine. I believe you know him."

With that, the buzzer rang to open the door that lead to the foyer

Frank and Benny had used to enter intake not so long ago. The look on Benny Robbins' face was one that Frank would cherish for a very long time.

"Benny...Agent Sandy Borden of the FBI. I know you two are old friends, but I don't think you're gonna like what he has to say one bit."

Chapter 67

Sara Evans and Scrappy sat on the curb in front of the Knuckle
Sandwich Deli watching the cars fly up and down Kingston
Pike. Having arrived early for a ten o'clock training session at the
deli, they both sat peering out into traffic waiting to spot Frank's
Concorde. They knew James would be excited to see them waiting,
eagerly, to learn as much as they could in order to help the deli
become a success.

Having no idea that Frank had been detained by Knox County's
finest, the two youths were a bit surprised when Rose James pulled
up in front of the deli alone. She always rode in with Frank. Rose
noticed the look of disappointment on their faces. She figured the
disappointment was due to the fact that they had beaten James to
work. A feat close to impossible to accomplish. He was usually there
hours before anyone else. She smiled at the two eager beavers.

"Well, it's nice to see you're both so excited to see me."

Embarrassed, Scrappy tried to difuse the situation and make Rose
understand that it wasn't anything personal. They had just been
hoping to score some points with the big cheese.

"No...Rose...it's good to see you. We just wanted Frank to see
us here waiting for him for a change. Ya know?"

"Relax. I was just playing with you. Don't worry, I'll let him
know you were both here way ahead of schedule."

"Why isn't he here with you? Has the training been cancelled?"

Rose wasn't sure exactly what to say. She didn't know how much
info to disclose at this point. Then she remembered the staff meeting

Frank held recently. He had been totally and completely honest with everyone and they rallied around him in his time of need.

She thought to herself, *why should this be any different.* Frank would want them to know the truth. With that in mind, she looked the two youngsters straight in the eyes and told them exactly what had happened.

Sara and Scrappy stood there astonished to hear that their boss, and friend, had been arrested. Their expressions changed from disappointment to worry to anger over the course of Rose's explanation of the past few day's events. When she finished telling her story, she looked over at the tears forming in Sara's eyes. Rose was amazed at just how quickly people became attached to her brother. It had always been that way as long as she could remember.

"Look here. We have to be strong now. Business as usual. So let's just march right inside and get ready to have a great day. Just think, don't you want to show him how much you've learned when he gets back?"

The two kids agreed. Sara wiped the tears from her eyes. Scrappy gathered his composure as well, trying hard not to reveal his sensitive side. He reached out his hand to Rose.

"Keys, please. Don't worry. Frank gave me the code to the alarm system."

Rose handed the keys over to Scrappy, allowing him to reclaim his role as dominant male. He opened the door and scrambled over to the alarm unit. The alarm light went from red to green as he punched in the code. 6-17-00. Frank's clean date.

Scrappy turned toward the girls to gloat over the fact that he was so capable. He didn't get the chance, however, as Sara let out a piercing shriek that sent chills down his spine. She became so ghostly white that it appeared that all of the blood had been drained from her body. With her mouth wide open, Sara slowly raised her hand and pointed toward the deli case that was home to all of Frank's homemade salads and desserts.

Scrappy looked at the cause of Sara's outburst and immediately vomited on his sneakers. His role of dominant male being short lived. Surely he would omit this detail when he relived this story in the future.

Rose stood weeping at the grotesque sight of Carl Metcalf's head perfectly placed in the deli case with a price per pound sticker directly below his chin. Whatever maniac was responsible for this had one sick sense of humor.

"Oh…Carl," she whispered.

Rose got herself together, grabbed the two teens and rushed back out the front door, hoping that their lives had not been permanently scarred from witnessing this atrocity. She placed the kids in the back of her car and scrambled to find her cell phone. Fighting back the tears, she dialed.

"911 Emergency. How can I help you?"

"I'd like to report a homicide."

Chapter 68

Benny Robbins' face was as red as a tomato at the peak of ripeness. There was no way that this could be happening to him again. How in the hell could his celebration be cut short like this. Just as he thought he was finally getting the monkey off his back by sending James away for good, the same bastard that let James off the hook some years ago had come back to ruin his life once again. What were the odds?

Clearing the final checkpoint, Agent Sandy Borden made his way over to Frank James and Detective Robbins. The gawkiness that normally was attached to his tall, lanky frame had disappeared. Anyone watching this man could easily see the confidence and sense of purpose exuding from every pore in his body. He was on a mission.

Borden maintained direct eye contact with Detective Robbins from the minute he entered the intake department. Though his face remained stoic and expressionless, Robbins could tell immediately that he was in for a major league ass chewing. The agent's long strides came to a halt in front of the somewhat cowering detective.

Robbins realized at this point that he had stopped breathing the minute Borden began his approach. Feeling a bit uneasy over the lack of space between the FBI's leading man and himself, Robbins stepped back, straightened his tie and took a deep breath. Not knowing what to do with his hands, he finally crossed his arms over his chest and prepared for the impending doom he was sure Borden was about to deliver.

"Benny, exactly what in the hell have you done here today?"

Determined not to show his fear, Benny puffed out his chest and stood his ground.

"What's it look like? I made an arrest."

"Under who's authority? You didn't contact me. You do remember the FBI has complete control over this entire investigation. And, whether you like it or not, I am the one they entrusted with the lead. Everything needs to be run by me before any action is taken regarding this investigation. That is, of course, unless you catch this sick bastard with the chainsaw in his hand! Everyone answers to me on this one, beause I have to answer to the powers that be. That includes piss-ant County Homicide Detectives carrying out a vendetta against a man he has chosen to blame all of his life's woes on."

"You make yourself sound real damned important, Borden. But, let me tell you something. All of the evidence has pointed to this piece of shit since day one. When I got wind of his print being the one your guys lifted off the picture they found on the O'Callahan girl's body, I figured that someone needed to get this menace to society off the streets before he killed again. I made a decision based on my years of police training and my experience in homicide investigations and I stand by actions one hundred percent. So put that in your pipe and smoke it."

Borden laughed loud enough for it to be heard by everyone in the jail. He was entirely pleased that Robbins had chosen to grow a set of balls right here in front of his peers. He could think of no better place to make this smug little worm look like the gigantic imbecile he actually was.

Borden cleared his throat.

"Sorry for that outburst, Benny. I just find it particularly amusing that you chose your police training and experience in homicide investigations to defend your position. See, I've done a little investigating in my time, too. It's been my experience that, when investigating any crime, it helps to interview important witnesses. Can we agree on that?"

"Of course. That's a no brainer. What's your point?"

"My point is, that in this particular investigation, you have failed to meet with any of the people who could help lead us to the real killer. You've not talked to anyone at The Katch One strip club, Spicy's or the authorities in South Carolina in regards to witnesses at the Corner Pocket. Each of these were the places the victims were last seen alive and intact.

"Fortunately for us, this man standing in handcuffs, did the leg work for you. You might have known that if you took the time to talk to this man, instead of using your sarcasm and idle threats. Would you like to know what we know?"

Robbins mumbled something under his breath and, with his tail between his legs, gave a nod for Borden to continue.

"We found out that the day Frank closed on his deli, he was followed by a black Cadillac Escalade with Florida plates. The inhabitants of that vehicle were two Hispanic men. Miss Sullivan was last seen leaving the Katch with four Hispanic high rollers. Johnny Tattoo was last seen partying and leaving Spicy's with two Hispanic gentlemen. The O'Callahan girl was seen flirting all day and finally leaving with…you guessed it…two Hispanic men playing themselves off as visiting golfers."

Not liking where this was going, Benny raised his hand.

"Now hold on right there. What about the phone calls? Even better, what about the photo? It had his prints all over it for Christ's sake."

"Well, Benny, I found out a little something about those prints. The photo turned out to be one missing from James' apartment. There were silver fibers on the picture consistent with the fibers on the frame that was missing said picture."

"This is all bullshit! This son-of-a-bitch is guilty and you're letting him off the hook. Just like last time. All this Hispanic crap is circumstantial. I'm not letting you get away with this."

"Look, Benny, you can complain to whomever you want on this. Just be prepared to have answers for all your inadequacies regarding this investigation. Believe me, they will be brought out into the open. If you really want to bang heads on this one, go ahead. I told you when I got here that if you tried any of your shenanigans, I would personally see you fry. I have no problem with you losing your job. As a matter of fact, it would probably be the best thing for the entire county."

Borden turned away from Robbins and unleashed his fury on the sergeant in charge of intake and release.

"I want this man uncuffed and processed immediately. He will be leaving with me and I will be leaving here in fifteen minutes. Any questions?"

Chapter 69

Within minutes, James was back in his civilian clothes, signing his discharge papers and receiving his property that had been confiscated when he arrived at the jail. It was amazing to see the jailers work together at such a frantic pace. It certainly wasn't the norm in this place, or any other county jail, for that matter. One would think they got paid by the hour, seeing how long it took them to perform the most simple of tasks.

Their newfound stealth and competence was, most assuredly, due to two simple facts. First, they seemed more than happy to accommodate the man who had, basically, just told the self-proclaimed King of Detectives, Benny Robbins, that he was a useless piece of cow dung right to his face. Each man present was, no doubt, envious of Borden for actually saying everything they had been thinking for years.

Secondly, although these redneck rangers liked to believe that their toughness rivaled that of a Navy Seal, they were, in fact, quite soft. With this fact in mind, it was obvious that none of these men and women wanted to incur the wrath of an FBI investigation that would, without a doubt, put an end to the very worker friendly environment they had created for themselves. It was like a whole different subculture was created inside the compound. A subculture based predominantly on inbred ideas formed in the foothills of the Smoky Mountains.

Frank James inked the last of a dozen signatures needed to complete the necessary paperwork the jail required to release an individual back into society. 'Necessary' being purely a matter of opinion. Most people would tag the repetitive forms ridiculous rather than necessary.

He glanced at Borden with a 'can we please get the hell outta here' look on his face. Borden was happy to oblige, having spent way more time than he wanted here already. Just as the two men were ready to escape out the door leading to the foyer of freedom, they were stopped by the familiar bellowing of Detective Benny Robbins.

Borden and James turned to see Benny storming towards them with none other than his cousin, Sheriff Tom Sanders. Both men stood shaking their heads, trying to decide if Robbins was either that determined or that stupid. Both James and Borden opted for the latter.

Sanders spoke.

"Wait one minute, Agent Borden. I'd like to have a word with you. Detective Robbins has told me what you're doing and I have to say I'm a bit skeptical myself. Don't you think we should detain this man until more facts come in? After all, we are talking about murder."

Borden sighed. He could see the obvious bloodline connection.

"Look, Sheriff. I don't know what half baked story your annoyingly ignorant cousin has told you, but I am thoroughly convinced that it is safe for me to take this man out of here with me. Surely you didn't get to where you are in your career by listening to every Tom, Dick or Benny with an uneducated hypothesis on issues as important and complex as this."

"No. I most certainly did not!"

"Well, that's what we have here. Detective Robbins is still whining over the fact that Mr. James was given a second chance some years ago. His opinion is biased. His investigation is an absolute farce. He has shown no signs of professionalism throughout this entire case. I urge you to think twice before jumping on his bandwagon."

Sheriff Sanders was torn between showing loyalty to his men and having the common sense to know that Agent Borden was speaking the truth. If word got out that he backed down, he could lose the respect of the entire department. If he didn't back down, however, he was in danger of losing the respect and support of the entire voting population. Basically, Sanders was damned if he did and damned if he didn't.

Fortunately for Sanders, he was saved by the bell. Ma Bell, that is. Borden's cell phone began buzzing like mad. He checked the number and apologized to Sanders, saying he had to take the call. Borden didn't do much talking except for a couple of 'yeahs' and a few 'uh-huh's'. He began rubbing his temples with fierce abandon.

"I'll be there ASAP," Borden said as he snapped his cell phone shut. He thought for a moment and turned to Detective Robbins.

"Benny. When exactly did you arrest Mr. James this morning?"

"We arrested him at 7:15AM on the dot, but I had a man watching him since midnight the night before."

"You sure?"

"One hundred percent!"

"Well, Sheriff, there's been another body found. The Coroner is putting the time of death at approximately 7:30AM. Give or take a few minutes. If what Detective Robbins is saying about a 7:15 arrest is true, there's really no way Frank James could be our man. Don't you agree?"

Sanders scowled at his seemingly retarded cousin.

"Yes, I would agree. Benny, I want you to drop whatever revenge scheme you've been plotting against Mr. James and get your ass to work on finding this madman that's been plaguing our city. Do you hear me loud and clear? You are to do whatever Agent Borden asks. If I get wind of any more nonsense, you'll be finding yourself scanning the want ads for employment."

Robbins nodded. He had just been handed another piece of shit pie and been forced to eat it. Life could be unfair like that at times, but it is hard to sympathize, for the misguided detective had brought it upon himself.

James grabbed Agent Borden by the arm, anxiously awaiting the name of the most recent victim. Praying to God it wasn't Tina, then feeling ashamed that he hadn't prayed for anyone else.

Borden looked down at first. Then, looking James in the eye, responded.

"I'm really sorry, Frank. They found the head of Carl Metcalf in one of your deli cases."

Frank James closed his eyes and wept.

Chapter 70

The ride from the Knox County Jail was a complete and total blur. Frank's head was spinning out of control. A variety of emotions wreaking havoc in his mind. Each one taking pot shots at his sanity. Up to now, James had tried to remain calm, cool and collected. With the death of his mentor, Frank was beginning to wonder how long he could stay on course. Knowing in his heart that if he allowed his rage and sorrow to take over, he would become his own worst enemy. Even more dangerous than the psychopath that has been stacking up the bodies of his past and present loved ones.

Agent Borden sensed Frank's torment and chose to remain silent for the duration of the ride. He was surprised by the strength James had been showing throughout this ordeal. Not only surprised, but also impressed. Impressed as to just how far this man had come since their first meeting a few years back. James had made the most of the second chance he was given by the Federal Government. A second chance in which Borden, himself, played a pivotal role in granting.

Frank's trance was broken as Borden pulled his sedan into the parking lot of the Knuckle Sandwich Deli. It was like a scene out of an episode of 'Law And Order.' Yellow police tape served as a barricade around the entire deli. Dozens of law enforcement vehicles, forensic vans, an ambulence and the County Coroner filled the parking lot. Out of the corner of his eye, Frank saw Rose, Sara, Scrappy and Marco surrounded by officers. He wondered exactly how long they had been there and exactly how much they had seen.

Agent Borden flashed his credentials to a uniformed Knox

County Deputy. They rolled to a stop near the dumpsters in the rear of the building. Instantly, they were bombarded by several plain clothes detectives eager for Borden's attention. Both James and Borden were escorted inside the deli.

Inside, the deli was buzzing with forensic experts trying to work their magic. Half dusting for prints, half using special infrared lights to expose various fluids that would otherwise go unnoticed. It was suprising that, even with all of the commotion going on inside the deli, the physical crime scene had remained relatively untouched.

Frank scanned every inch of the deli to see what exactly had been altered. He was surprised that the intruders had left the deli virtually intact. Then he saw it. Carl Metcalf's head was still inside the deli case. He had to fight back a wave of vomit. The forensic specialist scanning Carl's head informed James that the rest of the body was found inside the walk-in cooler.

Once Frank regained his composure, Borden questioned him as to what, if anything, seemed out of place. Amazingly enough, everything else seemed untouched. No locks or windows were tampered with. No money taken. There wasn't even any product missing. After assuring Borden that he would double check things later, Frank was excused to go to his family and friends.

James was greeted by tears of joy and sorrow. Joy that he was released. Sorrow over what had happened to their good friend Carl. Scrappy explained to Frank how he and the girls were the ones who found Carl. He was very thorough, except for excluding the whole 'vomiting on his shoes' thing.

Frank, in turn, recapped all he went through that day. From the arrest, to his short time in jail, to his rescue by Agent Borden. After letting them know that he was no longer a suspect in the case, he thanked Marco for keeping an eye on the crew until he got there. He decided it was time to get everyone away form all this bedlam.

Marco put them in Rose's car and watched them take off down Kingston Pike. With a smile on his face and ice in his veins, he soaked up one last appreciative glance at his posse's handiwork. His mind already beginning to concoct the next phase of his plan. He would go on a killing rampage starting tomorrow. His goal… to raise the death toll by five people in the next five days.

Chapter 71

Miguel strolled out on the deck of Calhoun's on the River, spotting his band of outlaws lounging at a large, square table along the back railing. It was a perfect place to enjoy the incredible spring day that it turned out to be. He knew very well that he had to reward his men for all their hard work. What better way to do that than to mingle with college students getting loose at happy hour.

Sandoval spotted his boss, called over the cocktail waitress and stood to welcome his friend with open arms. Javier and Troncillo followed suit without hesitation. Soon after, the men were enjoying appetizers and cocktails, appearing not to have a care in the world. Miguel regulated the amount of liquor ingested by the group in order for them to be clear headed enough to discuss business.

As the sun went down and the action on the deck dwindled considerably, the men settled in to discuss the course of action to be taken. Each underling knowing their role in the conversation was to listen and obey anything and everything Miguel told them. There would certainly be no opinions or objections, as was the case when they gathered to discuss the Metcalf murder.

Miguel began by applauding the work of his men. He was extremely proud of the fact that they had every law enforcement agency involved scrambling and scratching their heads. The only thing he was not pleased with was that the authorities had officially announced that Frank James was no longer a suspect in the case. He realized it was no one's fault in the group, as they could not have predicted that James would be arrested before the proclaimed time of

Metcalf's death.

While Miguel looked at this as a definite setback, he was confident it was something that they could easily overcome. The way they would turn this around was to perform a series of murders at an unprecedented pace. One a day for the next five days to be more precise. The list of victims consisting of, but not limited to, Mark Length, Rose James, Sara Evans, Agent Borden and Tina Gardner.

When Miguel finished his speech, he looked around the table and was met with blank stares and open mouths. He asked each man, specifically, if they understood their roles and if they had a problem with the plan. Each man answering yes to the first question and a resounding no to the second.

Another round of shots and beers was ordered. Upon completion, Miguel paid the tab and announced that he felt it was time for everyone to go home and get some rest. He exited first, not wanting to be seen with anyone as he left. That left Javier and Troncillo, who were dumbfounded, and Sandoval, who seemed to be unaffected by his boss' speech.

He stood, looked at his two worried companions and spoke.

"I don't know about you two, but I'm going to sow my wild oats tonight. I recommend you do the same. There's no telling how long it will be before we have this chance again. It could be our last chance if all does not go well."

With that, Sandoval turned and left Calhoun's, grinning all the way to his car. He knew in his heart that those two poor bastards were in for one hell of a night. Sandoval was amazed that there wasn't even a hint of guilt at the fact that he undoubtedly had just served up his partners to the wolves. He knew full well that they would head right to the Katch One strip club.

Chapter 72

I t seemed as though there was a gray cloud over the Flat Iron, the Alcoholics Anonymous club house located on Sevierville Avenue, as Frank pulled into the lot. Just as Frank expected, the place was jammed full of people, no doubt there to mourn the loss of one of it's oldest and dearest members.

Unaware of what type of reception he would receive, Frank closed his car door and trudged his way to the front entrance. Although the room was filled with the chatter of a dozen different conversations, the overall mood was quite somber. A mixture of sorrow for the death of Carl Metcalf, as well as fear for their own safety, had everyone looking for someone to console them and give them some glimpse of hope for the future.

All heads turned and all conversations ceased as Frank James made his way to the front of the room. There seemed to be mixed emotions in regards to Frank's appearance at the meeting. Some looked at Frank as though he was responsible for what had happened to Carl. Others feeling compassion for this man who had just lost someone very important to him. It seemed to Frank it would be only a matter of time before he was put on the hot seat. He was ready to put these people at ease in any way he could.

As the clock struck seven, a thin, gray haired man, with a face resembling a leather bag, rang a small bell at his seat at the head table. This meant that the meeting had officially begun. Next came the readings that kicked off every meeting. 'How It Works', 'The Twelve Steps', 'The Twelve Traditions', and 'The Promises'. At their conclusion, Leatherface paused for a moment to collect his thoughts. He finally stood, resting both hands on the table to support his frail body.

"Welcome everyone. As you know, this is where we normally ask for possible topics for tonight's meeting. I hope you don't mind, but I'd like to do things a bit differently tonight. That is, of course, if there aren't any burning desires anyone needs to get off their chest."

The chairman scanned the room looking for hands. When he was sure there were none, he started up again.

"I reckon the proper thing to do would be for us to have a moment of silence dedicated to our fallen brother, Carl Metcalf. Let us please do so now."

Everyone in the room bowed their head in rememberance of their friend. The only sound that could be heard was the sobbing of the congregation. God would surely have His hands full listening to prayers on this particular night.

"Thank you."

Along with the drying of eyes and patting of backs came a warm vibe that spread almost instantly throughout the room. Smiles broke out on the faces of a majority of the members, knowing in their hearts that it was Carl, himself, who was responsible for this calming effect. After all, why should his spirit be any different from the man that had warmed so many hearts when he was here in the flesh.

Leatherface began once more.

"I'm sure many of you have questions and concerns regarding the events that have been plaguing our city for the last few weeks. I know I do. Well, if y'all wouldn't mind, I'd like to ask the one man who may be able to straighten things out a bit, to come up and try and shed some light on the situation."

A hush came over the crowd as the chairman reached out his bony hand, gesturing for the man to join him at the head of the table.

"Frank, would you mind helping us out?"

Without hesitation, Frank James stood up and made his way to the podium at the far end of the head table. He felt somewhat intimidated as he looked into the eyes of this huge crowd of people, even though he considered many of them to be friends. Taking a deep breath, Frank reached down deep for the strength to continue.

Once again, he could feel his sponsor's spirit giving him exactly the strength he was looking for.

Frank stood up straight and asked the crowd to allow him to tell his story without interruption, assuring them there would be plenty of time for him to answer any direct questions they may have that weren't answered by his speech. He held the entire room captive as he gave his rendition of 'The Headless Horseman Killings', trying not to leave out any of the facts. His story lasted about twenty five minutes. Upon his conclusion, Leatherface announced there would be a ten minute break. After which, Frank would answer any questions. The room was full of commotion as people scurried to the bathroom, the coffee urn and out the front door to grab a quick smoke. Each one hurrying back to their seat so as to not miss one second of the action.

For the next thirty minutes, Frank was bombarded with a multitude of questions ranging from sincere to the absurd. He was forced to reiterate over and over that he was no longer a suspect, that he had no idea who was behind the killings and repeatedly urged everyone that was close to him to be very careful until this maniac was caught. No one who knew him was safe.

James felt like Joe Torre at a news conference after the Yankees had lost a World Series. Physically and emotionally drained from the inquisition. When it appeared as though the last of the questions were presented to him, he asked everyone to join him in a prayer for all the victims, as well as their families and friends.

Finally, the group formed a huge circle around the room and closed the meeting with the Lord's Prayer. When the last of the crowd had left the building, Frank sat down on the long wooden bench that framed the west wall. Never had he been to a meeting like this one. He felt like he was helpful overall, but prayed that he would never, in this life, have to be subjected to that type of pressure ever again.

Chapter 73

You could have heard a pin drop as the Escalade made it's way west on I-40. Both men torn between obeying their boss' orders and satisfying their own lustful needs. Amazingly enough, in these times of illicit sex, drugs and an overall decline in the morals and values of today's society, Javier and Troncillo were normally inclined to do the right thing. In this case, the right thing being responsible and loyal to their boss' cause. They would never have waived if it had not been for Sandoval convincing them to quench their own desires.

The excitement and anticipation that should have been growing inside each of these men were replaced with apprehension and fear. The primary emotion being fear. Fear based on the knowledge of what would become of them should Escobar find out that they disobeyed a direct order and ultimately put the entire plan in jeopardy. Neither of them had the slightest inclination that Escobar may have very well been the least of their worries.

As the drive continued, the two would-be playboys went over their game plan. The goal being to enjoy a few cocktails, partying with the girls and, finally, getting one or more of the strippers to leave with them. They checked their cash and cocaine supply. Satisfied there was plenty of both, each man filled a straw with the magical white powder. Javier took the straw's entire load to his head in one fierce blast. After shaking his head to clear his vision, he leaned over and took the wheel so that Troncillo could take his hit. Both men hoping that the man made euphoria would free their minds of worry.

Their apprehension was finally lifted as the Escalade turned off Lovell Road and the club's neon sign came into view. Relief at last. Grins broke out across their faces as they realized that good booze and young, nubile bodies were within their reach. There was no turning back now. They were finally struck with the anticipation and excitement that most men in their position would have had from the moment they decided to make the Katch One their destination.

Chapter 74

Agent Sandy Borden wasn't sure exactly what to expect as he positioned his tactical unit throughout the pot-hole ridden parking lot of the Katch One strip club. It had been his experience that anonymous tips were usually nothing but a complete waste of time. Some wacko wasting taxpayers hard earned dollars, as well as, precious time that could be utilized to find whatever maniac was choosing to wreak havoc on main stream America at any given time.

There was something different about this call. Somehow, this caller seemed believable. He was very secretive, offering a bare minimum of information. The mystery man wanted no part of any reward, nor did he offer any personal details that could help him be found should his hot tip pan out. He went as far as making sure his call was untraceable.

Agent Borden realized there would be plenty of time to analyze what made the mystery caller tick. Right now, however, he needed to concentrate at the mission at hand. He felt satisfied with the coverage his unit provided. There were three agents in the lot posing as drunken college kids, two cars on each end of the lot providing surveillance, two more agents portraying bouncers at the front door and a half dozen cars in the adjacent lot for back up.

Everyone involved was beginning to get a bit anxious, as the stakeout had been going on for hours with nothing to show for it. Patience was starting to wear thin. Even Borden was second guessing if he had overestimated the accuracy of the anonymous tip.

It appeared as though their perseverance would pay off as Agent

Borden's walkie-talkie broke the rather awkward silence. It was good news. The Sheriff's Deputy sitting watch at Lovell Road had just spotted a black Cadillac Escalade, with Florida plates, heading directly toward the Katch One as predicted.

Borden put his crew on red alert. You could feel the tension mount, everyone eager beyond belief to put an end to this madness. The lead agent's orders were simple. He preferred to take these men alive, but would not cry himself to sleep at night if deadly force was needed. The moment of truth had arrived.

Chapter 75

Sandoval took a long pull off of his Corona as he lurched in the shadows. He had found the perfect spot to park. There was no direct light hitting his car and he had a clear view of the entire Katch One parking lot. His ego would not let him miss out on seeing the end result of his phone call to the Feds.

Everything was going as he had expected up to this point. What a pure stroke of genius it was to make the anonymous tip to the FBI. He had spent the last hour watching the Feds scramble to get ready for their showdown with the two unsuspecting felons. While he had basically handed the FBI the men responsible for the Headless Horseman Killings, he was not one hundred percent sure that they would not screw up the bust. He believed that he insured the FBI's success by secretly stashing the chainsaw under the back seat. Once the Feds found it, case closed.

He closed his eyes for a moment, trying to muster up enough guilt that would allow him to say a small prayer for his soon-to-be ex-companions. The attempt was moot. Apparently his strict Catholic upbringing had used up his entire guilt supply at a young age. Besides, in order to have guilt, one needed a conscience. That was something his years as a gangster had rid him of completely.

Out of the corner of his eye, Sandoval saw the agents posing as employees sprint to take up their posts. The tall, lanky agent that seemed to be in charge signaled to the rest of his group to take their places. The action was about to commence. Sandoval finished his beer and replaced it with a fresh one from his small, travel size cooler. He hoped this wouldn't take too long. Looking down at his watch, he realized his date would be getting off work from Calhoun's any time now. Even the exciting drama about to unfold would run a distant second to another romp in the hay with sweet, young Ashley.

Chapter 76

The Escalade slowed to a snail-like pace. Concern broke out across Agent Borden's face as he wondered if his prey had been somehow tipped off to the trap that lay ahead. He radioed the backup vehicles to be ready, should the Cadillac turn tail and run.

Inside the sport utility vehicle, the two men continued to inhale piles of white powder in order to boost their confidence. They were completely oblivious to their surroundings. Once they had their fill of cocaine, the Escalade returned to speed and headed toward the finish line. It was time to party, and nothing was going to stand in the way of their good time. Or so they thought.

The SUV came to a stop next to a white pickup truck where the agents posing as college kids were getting into their roles. Van Halen blasting out of the CD player. One man holding a funnel, one man in the flatbed loading the funnel and the last man holding a stopwatch. Each one drenched in Budweiser from head to toe.

Javier and Troncillo got out of their vehicle and slowly walked by, staring at the drunken coeds. Playing exactly into their hands, the beer swilling agents went to work. The kid in the back of the truck lashed out at the two Hispanic men in his best southern redneck voice.

"Whadda y'all lookin' at? You best keep movin'."

Javier stopped and turned toward the truck. It was not in his nature to be spoken to like this and let the person get away with it. He was just about to challenge the orange clad youth when Troncillo grabbed his arm and whispered something in his ear. He was the voice of reason and Javier realized they could ill afford any unnecessary trouble in their lives. Javier shook his head and the two men made an about face.

Just then, redneck number two chimed in.

"That's right. You and your girlfriend get along inside. Have a few Cosmo's and do each other in the bathroom."

Both men stopped in their tracks and took a deep breath. They had to keep reminding themselves that nothing good could possibly come out of teaching these punks a lesson. Wisely, they chose to walk away once again.

Deaparately wanting the two men to come back and engage in a struggle with them, the redneck boy with the stopwatch decided to hit below the belt.

"Yer Mama's know they raised a couple of no good, faggot Beaners?"

Third time was a charm. They had struck a nerve with the racial slur. The two men turned around, placed their sport coats on a nearby car and strode toward the drunken bigots. If it was a fight these ignorant bastards wanted, it was a fight they were going to get.

Chapter 77

Agent Borden watched as the suspects turned to confront his colleagues. Everything was going according to plan. The backup cars were rolling into position with their lights off to conceal their advance. The agents doing surveillance in the lot began to close in as well. It appeared as though the scenario would play out as planned, with no one getting hurt.

Unaware of their current predicament, the two killers began a verbal assault on the college students. Just as they were about to charge the two closest to them, all hell broke loose. All vehicles came to life with lights blazing and sirens howling. Each of the pretend rednecks pulled their service revolvers they had hidden in the back of their waistbands.

The unsuspecting killers stood motionless as their world came tumbling down around them. Before they could make a break for it, there were a dozen agents storming at them from all directions. Both men got down on their knees at the urging of a tall man with an FBI windbreaker.

The two suspects were baffled why this was happening to them. They hadn't even fought yet. It didn't dawn on either of them that this could have anything to do with the murders they had been performing. They were more than confident that they covered their tracks. They thought their best course of action was to remain calm and act as though this was all some misunderstanding.

Agent Borden studied the two men, as his men retrieved the suspects wallets and handed them over to their superior. He went through each wallet looking for anything that would identify these men. There was nothing other than several hundred dollar bills in each. No license. No credit cards. Nothing.

The senior agent tossed the wallets to a short, stocky man with a dark blue FBI blazer and told him to mark them as evidence. Borden turned to the kneeling felons and began his initial line of questioning.

"What are your names?"

"No hablo inglais," the men replied.

Borden smiled.

"We know damn well that you *habla*. Should I play the tape back for you?"

The men still gave no response. It looked as though their identity would remain a mystery until their prints were taken at the Federal Building downtown. Then Agent Borden remembered the sport jackets these two removed before the confrontation. He directed the agent posing as bouncer to bring the jackets to him.

With one reach inside the left jacket pocket, the senior agent struck pay dirt. The first jacket belonged to one Javier Maldonado. Borden noticed some white residue on the corner of the ID, reached into the right pocket and pulled out a large vial of cocaine. Smiling at the perpetrators, he repeated the process in jacket number two. Another ID. Another vial of cocaine.

The suspects were actually relieved. They had faced drug charges before. Escobar's high powered attorneys would get them out of this with nothing more than a slap on the wrist. The grins that broke out across their faces would be short lived, however, as the FBI man dumped the contents of both vials on the ground right before their eyes. "Javier Maldonado and Troncillo Castillo, you are under arrest for the murders of Samantha Sullivan, Johnny O'Leary, Allison O'Callahan and Carl Metcalf. Not quite what you were expecting. Was it fellas?"

Javier began to *habla*.

"What are you talking about? Were not even from here. We came to this stupid town on vacation."

"Vacation my ass! More like a mission. You did well to cover your trail. We actually got tipped off that you would be here tonight. We don't know who it was, but I'm willing to bet it was the same person who used you to do all his dirty work. You two just don't look smart enough to be the masterminds behind this operation."

This time it was Troncillo who piped in.

"Fuck you, cop. You don't have shit on us. This whole thing is a set up so you look good in the papers. You just poured out the only thing you could have gotten us for."

"Is that so?," Agent Borden replied.

"Yeah, that's so. So get this show on the road. We'll be out by tomorrow."

Borden chuckled and motioned for the agent checking the Escalade to come over. He saw the terror in the eyes of both men as his associate came to a stop directly in front of them. They bowed their heads in defeat at the very sight of the blood-stained chainsaw.

Agent Borden squatted so he could look both of these men square in the eyes.

"There is no tomorrow for either of you."

Chapter 78

Sandoval chugged what was left of his beer and turned the keys in the ignition. He was feeling a certain amount of disappointment in what he had just witnessed. His boys didn't even put up a fight. It was probably for the best. They would have ended up getting themselves killed. Staying alive, they would be of much more use to him.

In all honesty, it would not have made a bit of difference if they had been killed. Sandoval would have had no remorse. He was incapable of that emotion. Nothing mattered to him except fulfilling his destiny. With the nights events coming to a close, he was one step closer to his dream.

He turned the car toward Lovell Road, leaving his headlights off until he was well clear of the crime scene. It was off to enjoy a night of frolicking with Ashley. He thought he had better make it a good one, because there was no telling when he might have another chance. The Feds were sure to make the connection between Javier, Troncillo and the Escobar family by morning. Then, surely, all hell would break loose.

Chapter 79

June 3, 2006

Frank James stretched and let out a yawn that resembled a lion's roar. He looked at the clock in disbelief, wiped the gook out of his eyes and did a double-take. There was no way it could be ten thirty. Not a day had past in the last three years that he had not been up by eight. Yesterday's events apparently had taken more of a toll on him than he realized.

Not only was he surprised by the length of his slumber, but also by the soundness in which he slept. It was hard to believe that he didn't even stir when Tina got up to get ready for work. *Why hadn't she said goodbye?*

That question was answered the moment he glanced over at her side of bed. Atop her pillow was a folded piece of paper sticking out from underneath a pack of cinnamon frosted Pop Tarts. Breakfast of champions. She was surely trying to soften the blow of her sneaking out without waking her man. It worked.

James unfolded the paper, noticing at once that she had dowsed it with her favorite scent. The message was simple. He was to stay naked until she returned. No questions asked. How could anyone hold a grudge after that? Certainly not him, even though he knew in his heart that he could not obey her simple command.

Propping himself up against his pillows in order to attack his breakfast treat, Frank reached for the remote on his nightstand and hit the power button. There was something about breakfast in bed with a little Sportcenter that was extremely appealing. Nothing, but nothing, could ruin the relaxing start to, what he hoped, would be a stress free day.

He couldn't have been more mistaken. Frank's jaw dropped when his television came to life. Right before him, live and in color, was a news conference set on the steps of the Federal Building in Knoxville. Standing in front of dozens of reporters longing to get the scoop, was Agent Sandy Borden. He urged the frenzied mob to refrain from pelting him with questions, so that he could give them an official statement. Once the crowd gave him their cooperation, he began his speech.

"My name is Sandy Borden and I am with the Federal Bureau of Investigations. They have assigned me to be the lead investigator in the Headless Horseman Killings. I am pleased to announce that, thanks to an anonymous tip received yesterday evening, we were fortunate to apprehend two individuals that we strongly believe are responsible for the murders in question. As of now, we are not at liberty to disclose their identities, as our investigation is not yet complete. I can tell you that we have substantial evidence to support the arrests."

The crowd of reporters began to unleash a barrage of questioning aimed at the veteran FBI man. Borden held up his arms, as he tried to be heard above the roar of the crowd.

"Please! Please! That is all the information I have available at this time. We will have a formal question and answer period tonight at five o'clock in the lobby of the City County Building. Thank you."

Frank shut off the tube. He sat astonished, realizing that any plans he may have had for this day were bound to be seriously altered. He raced for the shower, abandoning both his cozy bed, as well as his breakfast. He needed to get ahold of Sandy Borden and get brought up to speed on the case.

Tons of scenarios rattled around his brain while showering. None of them making any sense. He couldn't concentrate. He wanted... no... needed to know who was behind this and what his connection was to these psychopaths. While this information would give him some understanding of why this had happened, he realized that there would be a long road ahead before he was offered any closure on this whole ordeal.

Chapter 78

S andoval shook his head in disgust when Escobar came banging on the door of his hotel room. He looked at the clock and saw it was noon. They were supposed to meet at two o'clock to get ready for the next victim. His being early could only mean one thing. The news of the arrests must have been made public. Sandoval hadn't bothered to turn on the television. He was trying to get some much needed rest after his night with Ashley.

Throwing on a pair of shorts, Sandoval unlocked the door and let his friend in. Escobar stormed in the room obviously enraged. Sandoval would do his best to appear surprised at whatever the boss threw his way.

"Do you have any idea where Javier and Troncillo are?"

"In their rooms? Eating? I really have no idea."

"Have you seen the news?"

"No, I was sleeping."

"The fucking cops are saying they made two arrests last night. Something about an anonymous tip. They say they have evidence."

"What does that have to do with us?"

"I'll tell you what. Those two idiots are missing. The cops made two arrests. It's a little more than coincidence. Don't you think?"

"Slow down. We don't know it's them."

"The Escalade is missing as well."

"Maybe they went to eat."

"I've been in their rooms. The beds haven't been slept in. Do you know if they went out last night?"

Sandoval gazed at his feet for a moment. Slowly raising his head, he made eye contact with Miguel.

"I told them not to. I said to wait, but they kept saying they deserved it. When I left them, it appeared as though I had talked them out of it."

Miguel's face turned beet red.

"Those bastards! Exactly where was it they wanted to go?"

"That club. You know, the one we found Samantha at."

At that moment, Escobar knew in his heart that his two flunkies were in police custody. He couldn't believe they were stupid enough to go back there. This was bad. They must not be allowed to share any information with the police.

Escobar paced back and forth momentarily, then turned to Sandoval.

"Here's what you do. When they call, and they will call, you let them know that we will have our best lawyers here to defend them right away. Assure them that we will take care of everything they need and we will provide them with every possible convenience should they have to spend any time in jail."

"What if they don't buy it. Let's face it, they're looking at a murder rap. I'd say they would turn in a minute to get a good plea."

"That's why you tell them that we already have their families at our compound in the Everglades. Let them know, in no uncertain terms, that each and every one of them will be tortured and killed if they should decide to sing."

Sandoval knew he would do it. He hated that life meant nothing to Miguel. That's the way it is when dealing with those types of people. *Those types of people.* Sandoval had to laugh. He had to laugh to keep from crying, for ever since his parent's death, he had become one of those types of people. Perhaps God would forgive him some day.

He assured his boss that he would take care of everything. Escobar instructed him to sit tight and call him the minute he had something. As Miguel reached the door, he turned to Sandoval and spoke in an evil tone.

"You realize this changes nothing. These people will die. The show must go on."

Sandoval laughed to himself. The show would go on, indeed. Too bad for Miguel that he was no longer writing the script.

Chapter 81

F rank James wandered aimlessly around the deli. He was frustrated and annoyed that he was no closer to having any answers now than he was at home. His bid to get some answers from the Feds was denied as United States Marshalls, posted at every access point to the Federal Building in downtown Knoxville, were turning everyone away that did not have the proper credentials to gain access.

Frank was able to get Sandy Borden on the line, but was told to keep busy and that he would get back to him as soon as things lightened up on his end. That is what brought James to the deli. The place was a mess from the forensic crews that worked diligently, searching for anything that would bring the authorities closer to the killers.

Not knowing where to begin, Frank decided to call in some reinforcements to help get the deli back into shape. It had just dawned on him that his scheduled opening date was exactly two weeks from today. The deli's present condition would lead one to place the opening two months away, rather than two weeks.

Perhaps some social interaction would help to take his mind off his woes and put his thoughts back on the task at hand.

Marco was the first to show up to help get the deli back up and running. Cleaning the deli, however, was of very little concern to him. His main interest was picking Frank's brain to find out everything he knew about the arrests that were made. Marco was certain that Agent Borden would fill him in immediately. He needed this information in order to plan out his next move.

Marco grabbed a broom and dust pan and began his assault on the floor around the dessert cooler. Not wanting to appear exceedingly interested, so as not to raise any red flags, he decided to dance his way around the topic. Perhaps causing James to volunteer the desired information without having to come right out and ask for it.

"I saw that you slept in this morning. Apparently having your name taken off the most wanted list agreed with you."

Frank smiled.

"I'd say it took a little weight off my shoulders. I haven't slept that late in years. Normally, if I was in bed at that time of day, it was because I had just stopped partying when the birds started chirping."

"I took off early. Didn't want to, but I figured I might wake you up if I sat around watching some dumb shit on television. There never is anything worthwhile on the tube that time of day."

"Not true today, my boy."

Bingo. The bait was taken.

"Oh yeah? What made today different form every other day?"

Frank couldn't believe that there was anyone in the city that hadn't heard the news. He looked at Marco as if he lived in a cave, then smiled as he remembered that it wasn't so long ago that he lived his life oblivious to the world around him.

"They say they caught the killers last night. Well, they got two suspects anyway. They couldn't give their names or anything else about the arrest, except that they apparently have solid evidence against them.

"Holy shit! That's amazing. So, who are they?"

"Didn't you hear me? They couldn't say at this point."

"No, I heard you. I just figured that your FBI buddy would have filled you in. You know, so you can figure out why they were trying to make it look like you."

"Yeah, well it seems like there's just a little too much going on downtown for Sandy to give me the time of day. He told me to sit tight and he'd get back to me at his earliest convenience. So let's just get this place cleaned up. I'm hoping that just might keep my mind off the other stuff until I can get some answers."

It took everything he had for Marco not to show his

disappointment and frustration over Frank's lack of knowledge. His plan would just have to be put on hold. He had come way too far to have his entire scheme come unraveled because of this little setback.

Frank and Marco began cleaning like they were on a mission. Little by little, the rest of the crew arrived and the job was complete before they knew what hit them. With it's physical appearance in tact, the only remaining question was whether or not the public would be able to mentally overcome the fact that the killers chose to display Carl Metcalf's head at the deli. The odds were against it. However, morbid curiosity just may help the Knuckle Sandwich Deli to beat the odds.

Chapter 82

Agent Borden watched through a two way mirror as Knox County's finest took a shot at interrogating the two men charged with multiple murders. He could do little other than shake his head as he was dumbfounded by their pathetic display. If not for the fact that they had already gotten a positive DNA match from the chainsaw, these detectives would never have been allowed in the same room with the suspects.

Their sophomoric approach hinged on separating the two men and insisting that each had already turned on the other. This was supposed to get them scared into spilling their guts to try and get a deal. Unfortunately, that nonsense only worked on old episodes of 'Walker, Texas Ranger'.

Having already sent the suspect's prints over the NCIC computer, Borden would allow this useless questioning to continue while he waited for some positive feedback from law enforcement agencies throughout the country. He didn't believe that these two men were smart enough to concoct this murder spree by themselves. He had been around long enough to know that these goons were just enforcers. Muscle for hire. That said, Borden was hoping to find who these hired hands were affiliated with in order to find the mastermind behind the operation.

Earlier in the day, Borden thought that these two may give up a name in order to save their own butts. However, they slammed the door on any and all lines of questioning once their attorneys showed up. This led Borden to believe that whoever was responsible for sending legal representation to these two mutts, must have sent word, via the attorneys, that bad things would happen to them and their families if they chose to cooperate. This reinforced Borden's theory that others were involved.

If what Borden suspected were to be true, there was a chance that the murders could continue. This juicy tidbit of information would not, of course, be offered to the press. Even if new henchmen were obtained to continue the slaughter, Borden figured there would be a significant window of opportunity to expose everyone involved before the new troops were ready to resume the carnage.

Borden glanced at the clock in the tiny observation room and decided that it was time for the interrogation to end for now. He was certain the two suspects would rather be in a cell than to be subjected to Benny Robbins and his band of merry men. That certainly would be his choice if he were in their shoes.

The suspects were sent downstairs, while everyone else met in the conference room that had been converted into the FBI's dining room. Disgusted with the idea of another pizza party with the Sheriff's Department, Borden was delighted when a pimply-faced deputy entered to inform him that something interesting had come back concerning the prints they had sent over the wire.

Borden logged on his computer, sat back and ogled the response sent by the Broward County Sheriff's Department in south Florida. He clicked through a series of photos showing the henchmen with a variety of undesirable companions. While the photos linked these men with an assortment of unsavory characters, none seemed to make any connection with their present situation.

He began rapidly glancing at the seemingly worthless pictures until one shot, almost resembling a beer league softball team photo, caught his attention. Although he could not pinpoint exactly what it was, something about this photo had him believing he'd found the connection he was looking for.

Borden began correspondence with Broward County in order to find out what this photograph actually represented. It took less than five minutes for him to get a response. The e-mail said it was a shot of some key members of the Escobar Drug Cartel that pretty much ran all of south Florida.

He had heard several stories detailing the antics of the Escobar

Cartel over the years. From what he knew, they were a fairly violent group dealing in drugs, gambling and prostitution. They used several legitimate restaurant operations to cover up their illegal doings. There had been several attempts to take down the upper crust of the Cartel, but they ended largely in vain, with only some minor players getting pinched on minor charges.

Still unsure of the relevance of this photograph, Borden dialed the phone with the intention of getting ahold of the one person that he felt could give him the answers he was looking for.

"Hello, Frank? Sandy Borden here. I need you downtown as soon as you can possibly get here. I've got a picture of some south Florida heavies that I think may be the final piece of the puzzle. I'm betting that you can shed some light on this for me."

Borden smiled. Everything inside him felt like this was it. How he hoped that was the case. Nothing would please him more than to wrap up this case without anyone else getting hurt.

Chapter 83

M iguel stood completely stunned. He was barely able to respond when James asked him to stay at the deli while he went downtown. His throat was dry as a desert nomad's desperately in need of an oasis. Frank's words continued ringing in his ears. He wondered how they could connect Javier and Troncillo to the family business so quickly, as he was certain they would not roll over after their visit with the attorneys. The fact that Frank had not used the Escobar name led him to believe they hadn't yapped to the Feds.

South Florida heavies. Those were Frank's exact words. It had to be his family. Who else could it be? Anyone trying to steal the Escobar's thunder, anywhere in Florida, would be dealt with severely. Regardless of how the authorities managed to connect the two, Miguel realized that the recent turn of events would drastically change his attack plan. There was absolutely no time to take out everyone on his list. He needed to get to James and end this thing once and for all. A quick exit from Tennessee was definitely needed.

As the shock of Frank's news began to dwindle and Miguel was able to think more clearly, an evil grin began to appear on his face. The smirk was due to the reason why Frank asked him to stay at the deli. Tina was on her way there right this very minute. What better bait to use than her to bring Frank to his knees? He would be begging Escobar to kill him once he was forced to watch the torture and murder of his beloved Tina.

Looking around the Knuckle Sandwich Deli, Miguel was pleased, thinking that this was the perfect place to conclude this saga.

Reducing this building to rubble would make up for not being able to execute everyone on the list. The very thought of Frank's life coming to an end in the very place he thought of as his future made Escobar feel giddy inside.

So much for gloating. There would be plenty of time for that after this ordeal was over. This was a time for action. There was no telling how long he had to pull this off. His first move was to get Sandoval to the deli immediately. He dialed his cell and instructed his partner to pack their stuff and get to the deli at once, explaining that he would catch him up on the situation when he arrived.

Next, Escobar began to barricade both the back door and the side fire exit. He would take no chances in letting Tina escape before James returned. She was pivotal for his success. Finally, he stacked all sorts of dry goods, produce, cardboard boxes and anything else that would burn in strategically placed piles throughout the store. He would ignite several small fires before turning on the gas broiler and making his escape. Thus, destroying any and all evidence that he was ever there. The open gas line would assure that there would be no chance of saving the building.

Confident that he had left nothing to chance, Miguel made himself a sandwich and sat down in a booth overlooking the parking lot. The thought of all this death and destruction had gotten him famished. Besides, he would need his strength in order to satisfy Tina's needs before he did away with her. Miguel figured there would be no better way to make Frank James suffer than to be forced to witness the sexual pillaging of his dear, sweet Tina.

Escobar wiped his mouth, downed his coke and sat back, thoroughly enjoying the electricity surging through his veins as he watched Tina's car pull into the lot. The three years of torment and anguish he had experienced was finally about to be put to rest.

Chapter 84

Frank James took a moment to thank God and everyone else for allowing him to make it safely to the Federal Building. It seemed as though his Concorde was on automatic pilot. He couldn't recall any part of the drive from the moment he left the deli and turned onto Kingston Pike. Nonetheless, he had arrived.

Although the security remained tight around the Federal Building, Frank was able to penetrate it quite easily this time around. No doubt Sandy Borden's handiwork. Once inside, he was escorted by two agents to the sixth floor office where Borden was waiting for him.

Frank was greeted with a hearty handshake from the somewhat haggard looking agent. It was apparent that sleep had eluded Borden since the anonymous phone call that led to the arrests of Maldonado and Castillo. The two men made a weak attempt at exchanging pleasantries. The fact that this wasn't a class reunion, but rather a pivotal point in a murder investigation, left both men eager to skip the formalities and get right to the point. The adrenaline flowing through James' body helped him to break an awkward moment of silence.

"Sandy, I don't mean to be rude, but can we get on with this? My brain has been reeling all day long."

"Right. I guess I've been so busy that I didn't realize what kind of effect this whole mess was having on you."

Borden motioned for Frank to come around to his side of the desk, filling him in on what he'd found out about the photo.

"This picture comes to us from the Broward County Sheriff's Department. I know you spent a little time in south Florida, so I was hoping you'd be able to shed some light on the connection between the goons we arrested and the big wigs they're seen posing with."

Frank could feel his whole body beginning to perspire and his stomach turning into knots. He had spent the better part of the last three years trying to forget everything that happened during his stay in Florida. Dreading the thought of having to recall those emotions and relive those experiences, Frank realized that this discomfort may very well be what was needed to put his past behind him once and for all.

Borden continued.

"These are the mug shots of the two guys we arrested. This is Javier Maldonado and this one is Troncillo Castillo. Do those names mean anything to you?"

Frank shook his head no.

"Well, after studying these two, I found it hard to believe they were involved in this on their own. When their high priced attorneys showed up, I figured they were sent here by the real brains behind this. That's when I sent their prints out over the wire. I got several hits, but none made sense. Until this came in from Broward."

Agent Borden pulled the picture from a folder near the fax machine. Before he showed James the photo, he decided to test his knowledge on the subject.

"Tell me what you know about the Escobar Drug Cartel out of Miami."

Frank's heart skipped a beat. That name seemed to hit him like a ton of bricks these days. It hadn't always been that way. He had some fond memories of his time with the Escobars. Unfortunately, all of those memories seemed to have been erased by that one fateful night on the beach at the Pompano Pier. It was his last night in Florida. He could still hear the gunshot ringing in his ears if he thought about it hard enough.

Borden, noticing the cold sweat breaking out across his friend's brow, offered James a seat. He was apathetic toward Frank's pain and allowed him to regain his composure, certain that they were about to break the case wide open.

James closed his eyes and began to give a fairly detailed account of his ties to the Escobars. He mentioned his friendship and business dealings with Diego Escobar. The two spent a considerable amount of time together partying and living it up on South Beach. Frank offered up everything he could remember, short of the night on the beach that changed everything.

When Frank finished his story, Borden asked him a series of questions. Questions that were meant to help him tie in his past relationship with the Escobars to the recent murders here in Knoxville. As far as the two could figure, there was no real reason to believe that the Escobars had anything to do with the murders whatsoever.

Borden was shocked and confused that this appeared to be another dead end. Frustrated at having to go back to the drawing board, he tossed the photo on his desk and turned to the dry erase board listing possible leads. Just as he was about to cross the Escobars off the list, his train of thought was broken by Frank's plea for his attention. He turned to his friend in time to see him turn as white as a ghost.

Frank stood trembling while the photo sent from Broward County slipped from his fingertips. He was muttering sounds that were incoherent to his FBI counterpart. Finally, Borden retrieved the photo and stuck it in front of Frank's face.

"What is it Frank? What do you see?"

Frank's blood ran cold. Focusing every bit of energy he could muster, James raised his arm and managed to point at one of the faces in the photograph. He could not believe what he was seeing with his own eyes. The picture was quite clear. He noticed the two men in custody. Diego Escobar stood dead center. To his left, Sandoval, the one man he could not stand during his stay in south Florida.

It was the fifth man in the picture, however, that took his breath away. Right there, in color, stood the man he knew as Marco Belizzi. The man he took under his wing and into his home. The man no doubt responsible for the sorrow and misery plaguing James over the last few weeks.

Chapter 85

Tina was slightly confused as her Monte Carlo rolled to a stop in front of the Knuckle Sandwich Deli. Frank's car was nowhere in sight. She glanced at her watch. Five fifteen. Could he possibly have gotten upset that she was ten minutes late? That made no sense. Frank was one of the most patient men she had ever met. That was one of the things she fell in love with in the beginning. He was the first guy she'd been with that actually had patience to deal with the issues that wreaked havoc on her daily life.

She reached over to the passenger seat and dug into her purse to find her cell phone. The only way to see what was going on was to talk to the man directly.

Too many times in the past she had assumed herself into a frenzy. She had learned the hard way that opening up the channels of communication was the only way to avoid coming to misguided conclusions.

Tina was scrolling through her phonebook when she was startled by a figure peering in at her from the driver side window. Her nerves were quickly put at ease when she looked up to see Marco's warm, inviting smile. She thought to herself that Frank was truly fortunate at finding such a personable and loyal helper. Sentiments that would change considerably as the evening progressed.

The unsuspecting damsel in distress, not wanting to be rude, slid her window down and hung up her phone.

"Hello, Marco."

"Hey, Tina. How are you today?"

207

"Fine, thanks. I'm just a little confused as to why Frank isn't here."

"Well, you're in luck. I have the answer to that riddle. He was called downtown by his FBI friend. Apparently, there was some sort of evidence they had come across and they needed your boy to make sense of it. That's all I know. But, he asked me to wait here with you until he returned."

"That's sweet, but you don't have to baby sit me. I'm a big girl and I'm sure you have better things to do."

"Actually, I don't. I need to do some work inside anyway. Why don't you come in? I'll make you a sandwich. Frank will be back in no time. Besides, you and I never really had a chance to get to know each other. What do you say?"

Tina had mixed emotions. On the one hand, she felt a little uncomfortable about being left alone with a man other than Frank. She wasn't afraid for her safety, but rather how it would look to Frank. She realized that he would look at it as harmless. Her real problem was that, if the tables were turned, she would have some choice words for her man if she were to show up and see him alone with another woman. Chalk that up to some self confidence issues.

On the other hand, she hadn't eaten since breakfast. Her day was extremely hectic and she had to work straight through lunch to finish a project by the 4PM deadline. She was known to get a little crabby when she became overly hungry. Her stomach let out a tremendous growl, she looked up at Marco and accepted his invitation.

Marco helped Tina out of her car and led her into the deli. He was quite pleased that she had chosen to come in on her own free will. It could have caused quite a scene if she hadn't. None of that mattered, though, as he would have done anything necessary to complete his mission. He had a date with destiny and nothing, or no one, would get in his way.

Chapter 86

It seemed like an eternity since James was initially paralyzed by the sight of his assistant in the same picture as Escobar and the killers. Borden waited patiently for the numbness to leave his friends body. He had already jotted down several questions for Frank during this short intermission, but was torn between waiting on his friend or getting on the horn to local and federal authorities to try and locate this man.

As Frank snapped out of his fog, it was he who made the decision to put everything else on hold until Borden put the troops in motion. Sensing that James would not waver on this issue, Borden agreed and excused himself from the room. Upon Borden's exit, Frank collapsed in the chair with his head in his hands. Out of the plethora of scenarios that had bombarded his mind since the beginning of this nightmare, there was absolutely no way he could have ever seen this one coming.

Dazed and confused, James would have given anything to crawl in a hole and not come out until this entire ordeal was over. Actually finding the man most likely responsible for this mess was his sole source of comfort. Or so he thought.

Frank went from a glazed stupor to perfect clarity faster than it took a Ferrari to go from zero to sixty. In doing so, his body became increasingly rigid and his fists clenched tighter than he could ever remember. Reality came upon him like a tidal wave. The reality of his situation being that he had unknowingly put the love of his life in the hands of a cold blooded killer.

He streaked out of the office and hit the stairwell to the parking garage, not wanting to waste a single second waiting on the elevator. With his feet touching every third step, James descended the six flights of stairs in record time. Within minutes, he was in his Concorde and leaving skid marks as he sped off in the direction of the Knuckle Sandwich Deli. Praying to God that he would make it in time.

Chapter 87

Sandy Borden remained amazed, to this day, at how quickly platoons of men would be armed and ready to disperse at the sound of his voice. While the majority of leaders got off on that power, Borden simply marveled at the loyalty and commitment of his men. It was that respect for his fellow agents that made him so effective. His men would kill or die for him, knowing that they could expect the same in return.

In a matter of minutes, he had dispatched federal agents to Frank, Tina and Rose James' homes. The orders were simple. Shoot first and ask questions later. Borden was in no position to risk letting this maniac get away or allowing harm to come to innocent civilians, as well as his own men.

Along with the FBI, Borden also alerted the Knox County Sherrif's Department. He instructed Benny Robbins to deploy extra patrols to help find the mystery man posing as Marco Belizzi. Robbins was also to alert McGhee-Tyson Airport, as well as the Greyhound Bus Terminal on Magnolia. He also gave Robbins a direct order to personally swing out to West Knoxville and check out the deli.

Confident that he had done everything in his power to speed up the apprehension of the missing link, Borden returned to his office eager to put a name to the face in the photo. He stood perplexed in the doorway, wondering where James had gone off to. Turning to the agents remaining in house to man the phone lines, Borden questioned them as to the whereabouts of Frank James. He was met with blank stares. James appeared to have vanished into thin air.

Borden's internal radar was going off at full force. Something had to be desparately wrong for James to exit so quickly and without notice. It didn't take much for Borden to come to the conclusion that James was on his way to face the man responsible for trying to ruin his life. He didn't know where. He didn't know why. What he did know was that things were about to get ugly real quick. Certain that there would be more bodies to add to the death toll, he prayed, with all his might, that it was the bad guys and not Frank James.

Chapter 88

Tina glanced around the deli as she waited for Marco to finish her sandwich. An unspeakable apprehension began swimming through her veins as she noticed the random piles of debris scattered throughout the place. Striking her as more than odd, she nonchalantly strolled over to the pile placed in front of the rest rooms.

Carefully studying the contents of the mound, she tried to find some sort of logic as to it's makeup. Some of it was junk, while other pieces of it were clearly useful untouched product used in the daily operation of the restaurant. Unable to make any sense out of it, she turned back toward Marco to ask him why these miscellaneous mounds were almost strategically placed throughout the building.

Suddenly Tina froze in place. The unmistakable scent of gasoline had invaded her sinus cavity. Having recently filled her tank on the way over, she checked her hands to see if they were responsible for the odor. They weren't.

With her apprehension building into concern, she turned back to study the pile of debris once again. The scent grew stronger as she approached. With her concern now escalating to severe nervousness, she bent down to get a closer look at a dark stain covering the cardboard at the bottom of the heap. She touched her finger to it. There was moisture. As she brought her finger closer to her nose, it was apparent that someone had soaked the cardboard in gasoline.

Tina's emotions had now reached full blown fear. She lost the desire to question what was happening, wanting only to get the hell out of Dodge. She quietly got up to her feet and peeked over at the deli case where Marco had been previously working on her dinner. Luck seemed to be on her side. He had just put her sandwich on the counter, turned and disappeared into the walk-in cooler.

Everything inside her told her to hit the door and keep on running. Something rotten was going on here at the deli and she wanted no part of it. Realizing time was of the essence, Tina tiptoed to the counter, grabbed her purse and took off like a shot toward the door.

Her attempt at fleeing lasted only seconds. She stopped cold when a bright light hit her in the eyes. She stood there looking into the dark, evil eyes of a tall, olive skinned man holding a long, pearl handled machete. The light in her eyes had been a reflection of his razor sharp weapon.

Sandoval gave the lovely lady a toothy, but rather sinister grin.

"Don't leave now, *chica.* The party is just about to begin.

Chapter 89

I t was a Murphy's Law type of ride for Frank, as everything that could go wrong, was going wrong. His troubles began the moment he merged onto I-40 West. The traffic was thick, with an enormous amount of tractor trailers causing extreme congestion and speeds below forty miles per hour. James threw caution to the wind as he swerved in and out of traffic. Eager to eat up the miles separating him and the deli, the unsympathetic traffic allowed him to advance at a mere snail's pace.

To add insult to injury, several attempts to get Tina on her cell phone had resulted in failure. Frank's lack of control over the situation had him teetering on the brink of insanity. He hadn't felt this helpless since his using days. In the old days, he would have either thrown up his hands in defeat or been impulsive and overly aggressive, both of which would be unproductive and ultimately result in him getting high.

Frank realized, as he coasted just short of Papermill Drive, that it would be totally counterproductive to regress back to acting on his old behavior patterns. Drawing strength from the past, however, could be used to his advantage. This epiphany turned Frank's demeanor from uptight and reckless to calm, cool and collected.

Quickly assessing the situation, James swerved onto the shoulder leading to Papermill Drive, determining it would take less time if he hit the back roads than if he were to remain on the interstate all the way to the West Hills exit. He timed the light perfectly as he banked left and sped down Papermill on his way to Kingston Pike.

Within minutes, the deli appeared on James' left. His plan was to pass the plaza that was home to the deli, pull off the road and double back to take Marco by surprise. That plan, however, changed drastically as Frank's cell phone came to life. He looked at the monitor. It was Tina.

James eyed Tina's car parked directly in front of the deli as he passed by. Praying that she was there alone, he answered the phone. He was cut off before he could say a word by the one voice he didn't want to hear.

"Listen carefully. I saw you pass us just now. Don't try to be cute. You need to turn around, pull into the lot and walk ever so slowly in through the front door. Once inside, you need to turn and face the door, get down on your knees and put your hands behind your head. Do this exactly and no one gets hurt just yet."

"You son-of-a-bitch. I took care of you. How could you do this?"

"Let's get one thing straight. You took care of Marco, not me. He's not real. But believe me, I am. Don't test me."

"Let Tina go out the front door and I'll come in. We can settle this man to man. It's me you want."

"Shut up James. See, you are not the boss anymore. I am. So you don't get to tell me what to do. Get your ass in here in three minutes or I will gut this bitch like a pig. The clock is ticking."

James shut his phone as his heart sank. Things didn't look good. He said a little prayer for Tina, heartbroken that it was his sordid past that put her at the mercy of these barbarians. He wondered if she could ever forgive him should it be God's will that they get out of this alive.

Chapter 90

Believing, beyond the shadow of a doubt, that this psychopath would have no problem making good on his threat, Frank did not hesitate to make a u-turn right there on Kingston Pike in the middle of rush hour. There was no shortage of squealing tires, blowing horns and a variety of obscenities, both oral and digital. The front two cars in the oncoming lane were able to stop a mere inches short of becoming a pile of twisted steel.

Feeling bad, but having no time for apologies of any kind, James merged the Concorde into the right lane just in time to make the entrance to the Montvale Shopping Center. Pulling in front of the deli, he came to a stop right beside Tina's vehicle. He was fresh out of ideas. With no time left on the clock, Frank came to the fateful conclusion that he would have to count on Divine intervention to get him out of this one.

James rattled off a quick 'foxhole prayer', swearing to God and all that was holy, that he would never ask for anything again if he and Tina could just get out of this mess alive. If he had more time, Frank undoubtedly would have seen the irony in his request for help. Throughout his past, James resorted countless times to the same type of pathetic plea to get him out of some ridiculous situation he had put himself in.

All out of options, Frank took a deep breath and headed toward the door. He noticed right away that the shades were pulled completely down over every window and kicked himself for having picked such a dark color that allowed zero visibility inside. Peering through the front door, Frank was able to see Tina standing bound and terrified behind the cash register. Her eyes were desperately trying to give away the location of her captors.

Frank entered the deli and tentatively took a few steps inside. There was no sign of Marco, or whoever the hell he was, anywhere in sight. Sensing a potential opportunity, James made a move toward Tina. That attempt at disobeying Miguel's orders was rewarded with the butt end of Sandoval's shotgun connecting with the base of his neck.

The force of the blow knocked James to his knees. He stayed down rubbing his neck, realizing he was fortunate not to be knocked out completely. Turning his focus back to Tina, he was given a blast of adrenaline as Miguel stormed up to her and slapped her across the face. James was about to charge when he felt the barrel of Sandoval's gun pressing against the back of his head.

Miguel laughed.

"See Frank? See what happens when you disobey me? There are consequences. Not only for you, but for this pretty little thing here."

Miguel tilted Tina's head back and outlined her throat with one of Frank's own filleting knives. Softly kissing her neck, he continued with James.

"Now do as I told you. It should be easier now that you're already on your knees. Put your hands behind your head so that my associate can cuff you."

Frank hesitated.

"Do it now!"

James obeyed this time, never losing eye contact with the man threatening to carve Tina like a Christmas goose. He grimaced as the cold steel clenched down on his wrists.

Sandoval pulled James to his feet while digging the gun's barrel into the center of his back. He instructed James to keep his eyes forward and head toward the back of the deli. Miguel and Tina met them as they rounded the dessert cooler that recently was home to Carl Metcalf's head.

To be this close to this filthy animal, but unable to reach out and wring his neck, had Frank's blood boiling. He would give anything for a chance to turn the tables on these two ruthless killers. With no chance to physically alter the situation, Frank decided to try and get inside their heads.

Not wanting to admit defeat, Frank looked at Miguel. Trying his best to sound confident, James began to try and reason with him.

"You have to know you can't get away with this."

Miguel snarled back.

"Do not speak unless spoken to!"

"The FBI is on the way here as we speak."

Without warning, Miguel slid his knife across Tina's left cheek, leaving a small trail of blood sliding down her face. When she cried out, he backhanded her and shouted for her to stop her whining.

"Thank your friend for that. I told you there would be consequences. Keep your fucking mouth shut and I promise that I will do my best to answer all your questions before I am through."

James bit his lip to keep any further damage from happening to his girl. He was inconsolable it had gone this far already. As they trudged their way to the back store room, Frank wondered how any one man could become so coldhearted that he could knowingly break God's commandments without any remorse or fear of retribution.

Chapter 91

Agent Sandy Borden was going a little stir crazy seated in his sixth floor office of the Federal Building. It was totally unlike him not to be out leading the hunt. As soon as he heard from his men, eliminating possibilities of where this showdown would take place, he would hightail it from the office and be a part of the action.

Borden had, however, been making the most of his pencil pushing time. Since James' departure, he had received more feedback from Broward County.

They had been able to identify the fifth man in the picture as Miguel Escobar. He was the brother of Diego Escobar, who Frank was admittedly linked to.

The inquisitive FBI man was also informed of the night that Diego Escobar was murdered on Pompano Beach. When the police arrived, they found Escobar in the arms of his brother. Miguel was then sent to Broward County Psych Center, where he had spent the better part of the last three years. He was not allowed to leave until a board of psychiatrists were convinced that he no longer sought revenge against the man he thought was responsible for his brother's death. That man was none other than Frank James.

With Broward County basically explaining the 'why' in this case, the only thing left was to locate Escobar before anyone else lost their lives. Regardless of James' guilt or innocence regarding his brother's death, Miguel had crossed the line and there was no going back. He must be stopped.

Borden sat questioning whether or not he thought Frank could have murdered Diego Escobar. If it was not for the fact that the night of the murder corresponded exactly with Frank's hasty departure from Florida and his decision to give up drugs and alcohol for good, he would have dismissed the idea immediately. With this knowledge and his years of training, he had to admit to himself that anything was possible.

His cell phone rang, bringing him back to the issue at hand. The FBI dispatcher was on the line. He had received confirmation from each of the three patrols sent out to check the houses of Frank, Tina and Rose James. There was no sign of anyone at Frank and Tina's. The third patrol reported that everyone was accounted for at Rose's house and that they would guard them until this thing played out.

That was all Borden needed to hear. In seconds, he grabbed his gun and was out the door. It had to be the deli. He kicked himself for not going there to begin with. The fact that Benny Robbins was sent to check out the deli should have comforted him. However, Robbins' incompetence in every facet of the investigation left Borden anything but relieved.

Chapter 92

Miguel's body was tingling with excitement. He had waited nearly three years for this moment. The chance to avenge his brother's death. How he had longed for the chance to spill the blood of Frank James. All the planning. The waiting. Finally, the time had come.

As they reached the dry storage, Frank and Tina were violently shoved to the floor. Frank's head ricocheted off of a rack holding institutional size cans of ketchup and olives. Tina was fortunate enough to be tossed onto a mound of fifty pound bags of flour. She recovered first and crawled on her knees to Frank, still hoping that he would pull something out of his bag of tricks to get them out of this mess.

Miguel turned to Sandoval and informed him what he wanted done next.

"Sandoval, I placed some fuses under the front register. Put one leading to each pile of cardboard in the restaurant. They have all been soaked with gasoline. We will have fifteen minutes to finish up here before each pile bursts into flames. I have already turned the gas grill on low. By the time the fire reaches the deli case, this whole place will blow sky high."

Continuing in his subservient role, Sandoval nodded quietly and headed off to do his duty. Miguel turned back to Tina and continued his speech.

"Don't be scared, my dear. You won't feel a thing when this place explodes. I am going to slit your throat way before that happens."

Tina burst into tears, sobbing uncontrollably. Frank did his best to console her, but it was difficult considering his hands were cuffed behind his back. He glared at his captor wanting to assault him with some verbal venom, but he knew Miguel would find nothing but humor in his meaningless threats.

Miguel got right into James' face and looked intently into his eyes.

"I look in your eyes and see hatred and betrayal. That makes me very pleased. It has been my intention to bring you great pain throughout this entire exercise."

"Why? Why me? I never did anything to you. Hell, I'm not even sure who the fuck you are to tell you the truth."

Escobar pulled up a five gallon bucket of dill pickles and sat face to face with Frank. An evil grin broke out across his face, leaving him resembling the Joker in the Batman comics James used to read as a kid.

"I guess it is time to enlighten you as to why I am about to take your life. It's quite simple, actually. I've been planning your demise ever since you took my brother from me. Perhaps you remember the night you shot and killed Diego Escobar at the Pompano Pier?"

A look of astonishment spread across Frank's face. His stomach turned as he remembered back to that fateful night on the beach. Things started to make sense. Miguel's face was somehow familiar to him the first time he met him at the deli. Now he remembered why. This was the man who raced to Diego's side after his assailant fled the scene.

"So you're Diego's brother Miguel?"

"That I am."

"I hate to be the one to break this to you since you've obviously put so much effort into paying me back for your brother's death, but I'm afraid you've got the wrong man."

Chapter 93

Sandoval stood quietly outside the door of the dry storage. Reaching into a backpack, he pulled out three clear bottles filled with kerosene. He took the caps off of each bottle and replaced them with thin strips of white cloth. He wouldn't be needing the fuses. Too much work. Besides, he wasn't about to miss Miguel's little one man show that explained why he was doing what he was doing.

He found it hysterical when Miguel played the role of the tough guy. Nothing could be so far from the truth. Sandoval looked at Miguel as being weak.

He always needed someone to do the dirty work for him, using the excuse that he was the boss. In his eyes, it was his job to delegate the rough stuff. Sandoval was sure the real reasons were fear and the need to appear more powerful than everyone else. Miguel's vanity was the one thing he despised most.

Sandoval laughed at the irony of the situation, as Miguel explained to James how revenge was the motivation behind the events leading up to this much anticipated climax. It was ironic because Escobar believed he would be liberated by avenging his brother's death. He had no idea that Sandoval was acting out the final stage of his own little revenge scheme. Revenge aimed at the leader of the Escobar family. Hector Escobar, the man responsible for leaving Sandoval an orphan at such a young age.

It had been Sandoval's dream to get the chance to torture and kill Hector himself. That was when he was a child. As he grew, he realized that death would not nearly even the score. Not even close.

He longed for Hector to feel the unbearable sense of loss that he had been forced to endure as a child. A severe emotional void that had yet to be filled to this day.

Sandoval decided a few years back that Senor Escobar had to lose his two sons. That, and that alone, would allow him to finally be able to grieve his parents death and put it behind him once and for all. This whole thing could have been over three years ago, had Miguel not been locked up by Broward County. That worked to Sandoval's advantage, however, as he became Hector's right hand man in Miguel's absence.

Constantly remaining by Hector's side, Sandoval was able to witness his pain and suffering over the death of Diego first hand. Unfortunately, Hector became somewhat reborn with the release of his only remaining son. The pain seemed to have withered away. Hector needed to be reminded of the pain. After tonight, Sandoval believed Hector would be on his way to living in his own personal hell until the day he died.

Sandoval snapped out of his little trip down memory lane in time to hear James tell Miguel that he had the wrong man. That was his cue. It wouldn't be long now. He retrieved his nine milimeter from his shoulder holster. After putting in a fresh clip of ammo, Sandoval switched off the safety and prepared to finish the job he had set out to do three years ago.

Chapter 94

M iguel rolled his eyes at James' feeble attempt to make him think he made a mistake.

"What a shocker! Who would have thought that you would tell me I was wrong and try to beg for your pathetic little life."

Frank had had just about enough of this wanna-be gangster. He decided, right then, that if this was the way God had intended him to go out, he was going to do it with some dignity. This jerk definitely was in the position to kill him, but he didn't have the power to reduce him to a sniveling coward.

"Listen here, you horse's ass! Let's get something straight right now. I'm not begging you for anything. If you're going to kill me, I can't stop you. After all, you are the coward with the gun. All I'm saying is that your little quest for revenge will have been all for naught."

"Give it a rest. I know that Diego was supposed to meet you at the pier that night. He had been acting nervous all day long, so I thought it would be better if I tagged along. Unfortunately, he left early and I had not yet gotten home. As soon as I found out he was gone, I hopped into my car and raced down to the pier. Both of us know what happened next."

"That's where you're wrong. You think you know, but I saw what happened. Diego and I did do business, but we were friends first and foremost. He was probably the one true friend I had at that time of my life."

Miguel sat back to think. *Could this possibly be true? If it wasn't him, then who?*

"You're telling me that you saw someone shoot my brother down in cold blood?"

"That's exactly what I'm telling you."

"Tell me who. I demand to know."

"Someone you wouldn't expect in a million years."

At that moment, Sandoval entered the room with his 9mm Berretta drawn. He and Frank instantly made eye contact. Sandoval smiled at James as if to say 'go ahead, tell him'.

James looked Miguel square in the eye and said, "Why don't you ask your trusty sidekick what he was doing the night your brother was killed?"

Miguel dismissed the idea as ridiculous.

"Are you trying to say Sandoval killed my brother? You must be insane. He has been like a brother to me. My family took care of him after he lost his parents."

Frank decided to enlighten Miguel as to what he saw that night. He wasn't sure that he could get him to believe it, but he thought he might just be able to coax it out of Sandoval. Something told Frank that he was just dying to let Miguel know.

"Look, Miguel, I was supposed to meet Diego at the pier. Trying to be inconspicuous, I parked about a mile north of the pier itself and walked down the beach. I hesitated as I passed under the Pompano Pier because I heard people shouting. I cautiously made my way to the edge of the pier, but remained lurking in the shadows.

"It was quite difficult to see the faces clearly at first, due to the fact that the only illumination was coming from the moon. The voices, however, were unmistakable. Diego and Sandoval were arguing by the shore. Apparently, Diego was upset because he felt Sandoval was becoming lazy and a liability. There was some more screaming and then Diego told him to get the hell out of his sight. As he turned to walk away, Sandoval pulled out his weapon, called to Diego and shot him square in the chest.

"Imagine my surprise. I was about to go to Diego after Sandoval disappeared toward the highway, but that's when you pulled up. I stayed put for a while, but got a little spooked when the beach was swarmed by the cops. When I left the pier, I went back home, packed my shit and left Florida for good."

Miguel's head was reeling. His heart said no way, but James was awfully convincing with his version of what happened. After contemplating for a moment, Miguel decided his heart was right.

"There is no way he would do that. He doesn't have it in him. Besides, he has too much respect for my family. Especially my father."

Sandoval stood by quietly as long as he could, but that comment about respect was more than he could stand. It was time to shut Miguel up once and for all. Without warning, he walked up behind Miguel and placed the barrel of his gun to the back of his head.

"You ignorant bastard. This is how much I respect your family."

Sandoval pulled the trigger without hesitation or remorse. The bullet entered Miguel at the base of his skull, exited through his left eye socket and implanted itself in the wall next to James. Tina let out a piercing scream as Miguel fell face first onto her legs.

Sandoval tilted his head back and took in a deep breath. Killing Escobar appeared to have a rather euphoric effect on him. He opened his eyes as wide as he could. They looked as though they would pop right out of his head. Exhaling ever so slowly, he spoke to his hostages.

"That felt gooooood. So, who's next?"

Chapter 95

Sandy Borden weaved in and out of traffic like a veteran NASCAR driver on a mission to win at Daytona. He was shouting like a madman trying to direct the cars in front of him, not realizing that blaring his siren was doing the trick. The adrenaline flowing through his body was at an all time high.

With his eyes on the horizon and his pedal to the metal, Borden prayed that he made it to the deli before he was too late. He hadn't heard anything from Benny Robbins. That gave him a modicum of hope that things had not yet gone awry.

He began to feel a little better when he spotted a sign reading one mile to the West Hills exit. Another five or six minutes tops and he would be there. That feeling of hope dwindled rapidly as his radio came to life with the news of shots reportedly being fired inside the Knuckle Sandwich Deli.

Borden felt a wave of sadness creep through his body like never before, as far as work was concerned. He knew it was because he allowed himself to get too attached to Frank James. It couldn't be helped. He felt that he had a lot invested in the man and was incredibly proud of the progress he had made since being given a new lease on life.

Borden silently prayed to God not to take James from his life. It had been a long time since he had been able to feel emotions and believed, whole heartedly, that James was directly responsible. He couldn't help but think that Frank was sent his way to return the favor and give him a second chance at a meaningful life.

As he came down the exit ramp that led to Kingston Pike, Borden was slammed back to the reality of the moment. What seemed like a dozen police vehicles screeched past him with blue lights flashing and sirens howling. There was no doubt in his mind where they were headed. Borden accelerated and fell in line behind the entourage parading toward the scene of the crime, feeling somewhat pessimistic as to the outcome of this whole ordeal.

Chapter 96

While Frank was in no mood to beg Miguel for anything, his tune changed drastically as a pool of blue blood formed under Escobar's now lifeless body. He would beg now, but wasn't hopeful that it would do any good. James had seen Sandoval in action before. Cold-hearted and ruthless would not even begin to describe this soulless excuse for a human being.

James glanced at Tina, who was reduced to an hysterical pile of flesh and bone. He had to give it a try. Maybe, just maybe, he could at least save her life. With no time to spare, he began his plea for mercy.

"Why does anybody have to be next? You accomplished what you came here to do."

Sandoval smiled.

"Now Frank, you know that's not how these things work. You and the little lady are hostages. In this day and age, hostages never make it out of these types of situations alive."

"Hold on! It doesn't have to be like that. Nobody even knows you were involved. You could just disappear like that night on the beach. No one would ever have to know."

Sandoval's grin widened.

"It would be our little secret, huh?"

"Exactly. That way we all walk out of here winners."

Sandoval scratched his chin as if to ponder Frank's offer. After a moment of contemplation, he made his counteroffer.

"That certainly is one way we could do this, but here's the

direction I think we should take. First, I start by giving your girl a Columbian necktie. Then, I shoot you twice in the abdomen at close range. Very painful and very lethal. Finally, I arrange the bodies to make it look like you came in on Miguel as he was slaughtering your girl. You had a gun. He had a gun. He got off two shots before you blew his brains out. The cops come in and call it a triple homicide. All parties are accounted for. Open and shut case. What do you think?"

Frank could barely speak through the lump in his throat.

"I like my way better. We all live happily ever after and the case is still closed."

"The only problem I have with that is there would always be a chance that you or your friend here could get a change of heart and turn me in. Even though I'm sure you two would promise not to do that, it is much too big a risk for me to take. If we use my way, I walk away clean and never have to look over my shoulder again. If you take the time to look at it from my standpoint, I'm really left with little choice."

Frank bowed his head and began to grovel at Sandoval's feet.

"Please. Do what you have to do to me. Just let her go. She's got nothing to do with this. Please. For the love of God, have a heart."

Sandoval smirked as he approached James.

"That's very touching. You really love her, don't you. I'll tell you what. I can't let her go. But, I like you. You've been through enough these past couple of weeks. I'm going to demonstrate that heart you were speaking of by not making you watch me slice her throat. Perhaps you'll be able to remember her the way she is right now when you reach the afterlife."

With that, Sandoval leaned Frank against the ketchup rack, picked up Miguel's gun and placed it to his midsection. He looked at Tina and suggested that she close her eyes. Leaning close to Frank's ear, Sandoval whispered for God to have mercy on his soul. He closed his eyes, took a deep breath and began to pull the trigger.

A loud boom erupted throughout the room. Tina screamed at the top of her lungs. Frank clenched tightly, waiting for the pain to hit. Seconds flew by without any pain whatsoever, leaving frank confused. He opened his eyes ever so slowly and took a look at his gut. Nothing. No blood. No bullet holes. Nothing.

James trepidatiously raised his head. He saw Sandoval wide eyed, with a trickle of blood rolling down the corner of his mouth. Something caught his attention out of the corner of his eye. He could not believe his eyes as he focused on the smoking gun in the doorway.

Standing there, equally as surprised as James, was the most improbable of heros. Detective Benny Robbins, the man dedicated to destroying Frank James, had just shocked the world by saving his life.

Epilogue

July 2, 2006

gent Sandy Borden turned off Kingston Pike into the parking lot that had recently belonged to the Knuckle Sandwich Deli. It had been nearly a month since he was last here. He spent that time wrapping up the investigation of the Headless Horseman murders.

The deli had seen better days. The place once touted as being the next hot Knoxville eatery, had become just another casualty of war in the restaurant business. It's bright future snuffed out before Frank even had a chance to serve his first customer. The powers that be decided to pull their money and cut their losses. They felt it would cost too much to repair the damages that the deli incurred at the hands of Miguel Escobar. That, coupled with the stigma left on the building after the final blood bath that ended the recent horror which plagued the town, left a sour taste in the mouths of the investors.

Frank was cleaning out the last of his things when Borden entered the building. The two men had promised to keep in touch, but neither had made an attempt to do so until now. There were no hard feelings as both men realized they each had obligations to fulfill and, perhaps, needed a little time to recover from the recent events that drained their lives both mentally and physically.

James was happy to see a friendly face. His world became rather lonely after the decision was made to close the deli. That loneliness, however, was more or less self induced. He chose to be by himself, rather than have to be the object of people's pity or having to face the unending inquisition of what he would do next.

Frank started the conversation.

"If you're here, who the hell is out there catching bad guys?"

"I caught 'em all," Borden replied.

"I'm glad to find you here. I thought you might be at Benny's house. Figured he'd have you washing his car or something to pay him back for saving your ass."

Frank laughed.

"Touche."

The two men filled each other in on what had been happening in their lives. Borden gave his condolences on Frank's losing the business without the usual pitiful undertones. He asked if Frank and Tina were still together and how she was doing after her strenuous time with Escobar.

Frank assured him that she was rebounding nicely and they were talking about marriage. Unfortunately she, along with everyone else, was wondering what the hell he was going to do with himself.

"Do you have any plans?", Borden asked.

"Not a clue. This was my dream. I don't think I could go back to doing it for someone else. But, it's a little late in life for a career change. Besides, who's gonna give me a chance with my track record?"

"Well, that's kind of why I'm here. Thanks to your research in the case, I returned to Washington and received all sorts of accolades. They decided to give me my own special task force dealing entirely with mass murderers and serial killers. They gave me the authority to hand pick my own team."

James was confused. Why was he telling him this? What did that have to do with his prospects in the future? Borden read the look on James' face and continued to try and spell it out for him.

"You showed a natural ability to ask the right questions and have the kind of personality to get people to open up to you. That is crucial to success in my line of work. I know you're still raw, but we do offer a rather comprehensive training program."

"Hold on a minute! Are you asking me if I want a job?"

"I ran it past the Director and he told me to use my discretion. My gut says you could be great at this. Think about it. Talk it over with Tina, because it takes a big commitment from her as well as you. You know how to get in touch with me."

With that, Borden shook Frank's hand and was gone just like that. When the shock wore off, Frank found himself both flattered and amused. Flattered that someone like Borden had that type of faith in him. Amused when he thought about going from being wanted by the FBI, to being employed by them.

With no idea what he would do and no intention of deciding right away, Frank went back to packing. As he stuffed some useless office supplies in an old French fry box, he was amazed at how, when one door closed, another opened up as long as you continue to do the next right thing.

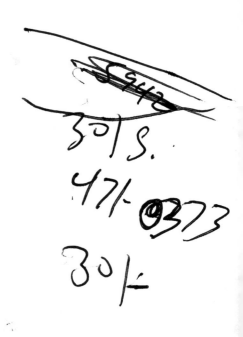

CPSIA information can be obtained
at www.ICGtesting.com
Printed in the USA
BVHW04s1832070818
523833BV00007B/214/P